The Cosmopolitan Girl

The

M. Evans & Company, Inc. / New York, N.Y. 10017

COSMOPOLITAN Girl

ROSALYN DREXLER

M. Evans and Company titles are distributed in
the United States by the J. B. Lippincott Company,
East Washington Square, Philadelphia, Pa. 19105,
and in Canada by McClelland & Stewart, Ltd.,
25 Hollinger Road, Toronto M4B 3G2, Ontario

Design by Joel Schick

Manufactured in the United States of America
1 2 3 4 5 6 7 8 9

LIBRARY OF CONGRESS CATALOGING IN PUBLICATION DATA

Drexler, Rosalyn.
The Cosmopolitan girl.

I. Title.
PZ4.D778Co [PS3554.R48]   813'.5'4   74-23526
ISBN 0-87131-169-0

THIS BOOK IS DEDICATED TO

Emma Licht

WHO TAUGHT AT PUBLIC SCHOOL 94 IN THE BRONX,
AND WHO ENCOURAGED ME TO WRITE.

WANTED: a dog that neither barks nor bites, eats broken glass and shits diamonds.

Goethe

. . . Dogs are relevant in connection with human society either because they suggest it by their own social life (which men look on as an imitation of theirs), or alternatively because, having no social life of their own, they form part of ours.

Levi-Strauss

One of the reasons I have always tried to perfect the way I look is that I thought it would make me happier.

Princess Luciana Pignatelli

The Cosmopolitan Girl

1   Pablo has confessed his love for me. I was stunned. I knew that he was fond of me, the way he licked my hand and slept at the foot of the bed barely moving so as not to disturb me. But a declaration of love! And from a dog I have owned for two years. . . . My God! I couldn't understand such an explosion. It is true I love him too, in another way, as a welcome responsibility, as a presence. Let me explain. I live alone. The room in which I live is located in the Hotel Buckminster. Pets are not allowed, but I have hidden Pablo. He is paper-trained and never barks above a whisper. He has a fine suit of clothes: wide velvet trousers, Hawaiian shirt, gaucho hat, and a wig. This is the disguise he wears should I have to open the door to anyone. When this happens he sits with his back to the door looking out the window. He is an intelligent dog, well coordinated and faithful (that goes without saying). I keep him with me to satisfy a desire that is so personal I am ashamed to admit it. My purpose is to tie together the two aspects of my nature: the civilized and the animal. However, Pablo is fast becoming more civilized than I am. He insists that a daily schedule of activities be read to him each morning, and that I present the day's menu to him for his approval. His menu might read as fol-

THE COSMOPOLITAN GIRL

lows: fresh chopped sirloin steak au jus (served in medium bowl on a lace place mat on the floor), mineralized spring water over ice (served in crystal tumbler), crisp burgundy vitamin capsule, hand-carved unpolished bone of beef. His menu is always at variance with the actual fare, but the captive customer's complaints fall on deaf ears and an empty pocketbook. Since he is in the habit of having me read the news to him while he eats, I change it in the telling to amuse both of us, for instance: "RELIGION REPORT . . . VATICAN ABOLISHES THE TONSURE. Pope Eccles XXIV today ordered the abolition of the tonsure, the circular shaving of the crown of the head that has marked preliminary steps on the way to a nit-free scalp. The Pope also maintained the age-old ban on women in any barberic role, emphasizing once again the moral contained within the biblical tale of Samson and Delilah. . . . LOCAL NEWS—HELEN JONES ADDRESSES THE P.B.A. Warning that corruption among the police, prosecutors, and judges must be confronted 'in a darkened, sealed tunnel,' Helen Jones today told the Patrolmen's Benevolent Association that she was afraid of rats. This was the first public indication that she was no longer interested in being a foil for the bigwigs. Despite the resentment of the governor, the mayor, and a state senator, she won three rounds of applause and an Italian salami for her decision to withdraw. 'I have lost confidence in our system,' she declared in the section of her speech dealing with misbegotten dollars and high cholesterol lunches for jurors, 'but I have gained my own self-respect.' For this she received a standing ovulation that lasted for five days, though with diminishing intensity for the last two." Pablo does not laugh easily. I keep trying. If he left me, life would not be worth living.

2

I am a pretty person. My features do not fight with one another. I have a small nose that is slightly rounded at the tip, adequate nostrils, and a flat bridge which might be more interesting should a bump appear along its bony path. My breasts are small, my spine straight, my thighs not much fuller than my calves. My color is good; I like to be out-of-doors. I try to achieve some excitement in my appearance by changing the way I do my hair (according to the way women in *Cosmopolitan* do theirs: natural but controlled, parted on the left side, falling in gentle waves to just below the ear.) My clothes can be mixed and still belong together since none of the colors clash, and they are classically simple. This is necessary since I have few clothes, and they must go everywhere: shopping, on-the-town, job hunting, man hunting (formal or informal). What I wear decides who I am. This is elementary psychology, but true. I once wore a tiger-striped nightgown and clawed a man to death.

At home I walk around with no clothes on at all (depending on whether the steam is up). I do not bother to pull down the shade. If someone in the building opposite wants to look, he's welcome. If someone doesn't like it, that's his problem. I do what makes me feel good . . . but not always. It's a hard rule to follow because sometimes I'm not sure what does please me.

3 I was about to go into my room when I heard Pablo ask: "Is it you, Helen?" Who else could it be? When I entered he claimed that he had had a bad dream. Then lowering his voice: "It was about the courtyard."

Our window faces the side entrance. Pigeon droppings encrust the court. One must step gingerly over the concrete to reach the door. The building was built in 1904. At that time it was the most elegant residential hotel in the nation, a huge edifice modeled on Stanford White's Beaux Arts school. Unlike the paper-thin walls of today's more modern constructions, the Buckminster has thick vaultlike walls. Stars of the music world like Caruso, Toscanini, Chaliapin, Jenny Lind, the Pied Piper, and Stravinsky found they could practice here without disturbing their neighbors. Privacy was assured. A good place for a murder.

"I dreamt I was lying in the courtyard dead," Pablo whispered.

"Oh no!"

"You're crying, Helen. Oh now, is it anything to cry about? It was only a dream."

I blew my nose without answering. There followed a deep silence. "I'll have to ask Mother what it means," I said.

4   Mother is a psychic; she can guess the past, present, and future. She does not believe it is guessing. She has spoken to more than fifty people with some degree of accuracy by merely holding a folded piece of paper in her hand on which they have written a question. When she speaks to me she is less accurate, since what she says is colored by emotion. The surgeon does not operate on his family, the seer does not tell a loved one what is in

| 17

store for her; however, Mother is the exception to the rule. I take what she says with a grain of salt. I am aware of her shortcomings.

Mother rose above me in the chapel, her batwing sleeves stirring the incense in the air. Candles flickered on the altar. The cross was wound with artificial flowers. A hymn began to play as one of Mother's assistants activated her new quadraphonic sound system. I was the only customer, but got the full treatment. Mother took the microphone: "Good evening, I am the Reverend Myra Jones, and I believe I can be of some help to you, if you sincerely seek it. . . ."

From my cushion on the floor I called: "I'm sincere, Mother."

She pressed the microphone to her lips and said tenderly: "Our purpose here is devotion to the good and natural things of life. You are what you breathe, what you eat, and who you choose to love."

Albert, Mother's chief assistant, took the photo of Pablo that I had put into an envelope. The envelope was sealed. Albert brought the envelope to Mother. She smoothed it between her hands, then held it very still. Her head went back and her eyes closed. She began to bark. Her neck snapped forward as she lifted the envelope above her head. Albert replaced the microphone in its stand. Mother moaned, sang a line from "How Much Is That Doggie in the Window," opened her eyes wide, and staring at me said: "I hold in my hand a picture of someone called Pablo. This is not the picture of Pablo Casals, cellist deceased, nor is it the picture of Pablo Picasso, artist deceased; this Pablo has no last name and no great talent though he is able to dance some, howl at the moon, run a fair race, or catch a well-aimed ball in his mouth. This is an odd sort of man who can achieve peace and tranquillity only by being free, this means sexually, and, let me see, he loves combat and is very strong. Yes, he is a fighter. One of his ears is slightly chewed, and his left leg is healing from a bite. What a purely primitive person! Oh dear. . ."

Mother made a circle with the envelope, then held it out flat on her palm.

"Tell me about Pablo's dream, Mother. That's what I came to find out."

"Please call me Reverend when I am acting in that capacity," Mother warned, "or my powers might wane."

"Yes, Reverend Jones. I apologize."

This time Mother began howling as she crawled all around the lectern with the envelope in her mouth. She was too far gone for me to think she was putting me on. I think that the spirit of Pablo had possessed her and that she was actually at that moment a dog. As a dog she was surprisingly appealing. Albert, putting his hands under her armpits, helped her up as she was about to speak again: "I receive an image of a dog lying very still. He is under a canopy. It is raining. The dog is Pablo."

"Is he dead? Is he dead?" I cried out, horrified.

"The dog is an actor. He is making a movie in which he is pretending that he is dead. It is not really raining but it is wet enough. Pablo will get a cold from which he will recover."

"But what does the dream mean, Reverend? Please tell me."

"The meaning manifest in this dream, which is the dream of a dog, a dog-faced man, or a man dreaming he is a dog, is that in grave situations one must laugh loudly, if need be, a great hollow laugh."

"I don't get it," I said. "There was no one laughing in the dream. The only sound was of the rain falling."

"Well, then, maybe the dream means that it is better to dream one is dead than to actually die. Your dog is suffering from extreme anxiety. One can surmise that from the fixed smile on his face, and the nervous twitching of his tail."

"Do you have any advice for me?" I knew that Myra Jones was wrong about Pablo's tail, he was a happy tail-wagger, not a nervous tail-twitcher, but she was right about his engraved finky smile. It drove me wild sometimes.

"Brush him often, play with him, and never tell him he's growing old. Also laugh a lot when you're around him. He needs reassurance."

"Is that all, Reverend Jones?"

"Oh yes, keep the bottoms of your windows closed."

Mother threw me a daisy which landed in my lap. She then disappeared into the black drapes that separated the chapel from the rest of the apartment. It was a magical departure. Music swelled. Rosy lights caused misty halos to glint off antique icons. Albert brought me an ancient silver wine bowl to dip my cup into. It was very peaceful. As I squatted on the pillow, sipping wine, I could understand how people would want to stay rooted in their places all their lives.

As I was leaving, Albert approached me: "I must see you soon," he said urgently.

"You know where to get in touch with me," I replied.

5 A bright cool afternoon, but Pablo was restless. I could have spent all day looking out the window at the blue shadows of buildings.

"I'm a dog," Pablo began, "and it isn't fair to keep me locked up in this room like an abused child some adult is ashamed of. Don't you know what life is all about?" he growled.

"Tell me," I said curtly.

"Life is fighting for territory, smelling another dog's shit and knowing it's not yours, pissing high on the tree trunk, and fucking a bitch! That's what life is all about. I love you but you're not enough."

"If you go I'll never see you again. You aren't registered with the city. You haven't had your shots, and you know you won't eat scraps."

"I'll take my chances," Pablo answered. He was really in a terrible mood.

I let him go, but followed him. As soon as he disappeared down the hall, he turned back again.

"I can't do it," he said. "An invisible force wants to keep me here."

"Remember, I gave you your chance," I told him, relieved.

6 Pablo has been angry with me since his attempted freedom. It would have been better had I refused his request. Someday I'll prepare him for going: walk with him short distances, let him run without a leash, call him back. Does a dog know what a dog wants? Without me he would be alone in the world, hungry, running with the pack (as do summer colony rejects); he'd become vicious,

a killer . . . indiscriminate. On meeting me alone some winter day, would he rip me apart to wallow in my warm blood? He was snuggled up against me on the bed, his wet nose stamping my inner arm with sticky goodwill.

"Tell me another story about Tommy the Turd," Pablo said. It was his favorite antihero tale. (Tommy the Turd appealed to his nose.)

I opened an imaginary book and read: "One day Tommy the Turd went out looking for a friend because he was very lonely. Now you know how hard that might be because even before you saw him you could smell him. But Tommy wrapped himself in a shiny new Saran Wrap jacket and went out into the world anyway in his brave quest for a friend. He visited the Museum of Modern Art, and was standing near the pool looking at his dark reflection when a curator of the museum noticed him. 'My, my, what a fine work of art that is!' the curator said to himself. 'I must have it installed immediately.' But first, of course, he had to ask Tommy whether he would allow himself to be installed. So he began: 'I'd like to be your friend. What is your name?' 'Tommy, sir,' Tommy the Turd answered, wisely leaving off his last name. 'Well, pleased to meet you, Tommy. I think you are a wonderful sight to behold and know that you could give pleasure to thousands of people who visit our museum every year.'

" 'How?' Tommy inquired innocently.

" 'By letting us install you in our permanent collection,' the museum curator replied. When Tommy hesitated, too overcome by emotion to answer, the curator misinterpreted and offered Tommy two passes to the museum which included openings and free movie shows for a year.

" 'Who would I give them to?' Tommy asked.

" 'Your parents? Friends?'

" 'You're my only friend, sir, and my parents have long since passed away.'

" 'I'm sorry to hear that,' the curator said, 'but as your only friend I recommend that you put yourself in my hands. You'll not only be famous, you'll be happy surrounded with other works of art and also people. You'll never be lonely. Sometimes there is music in the courtyard, sometimes poetry readings. Your spirit will soar.'

"Tommy, having received an offer he couldn't refuse, accepted and was put on a pedestal right in the middle of the pool. Beams of colored lights played around him, bouncing off the shiny Saran Wrap jacket like sparks of new stars. For one moment he was happy, then the fountain went on. The lively water found him under his fragile wrapper, and Tommy the Turd began to dissolve. The pool in which he stood changed from bright blue to a dirty camel's-hair brown. People who had been drinking champagne beside the pool to celebrate the new acquisition left with undue haste as the odor of decaying matter wafted toward them.

24 |

" 'Everyone's abandoning me,' Tommy cried. 'I'm nothing but a piece of shit!' When he disappeared, there was nothing left in the pool but a soggy scrap of Saran Wrap, which a workman scooped out.

" 'Excrement as art is valid,' the curator insisted, and there were some who believed him, artists who found a way to preserve their turds. But it was too late for Tommy."

Pablo brushed a tear from his eye: "If only Tommy had realized that there are more turds in the world than people, he would have had a sense of pride," he said, "but he did have his moment of glory."

"Yes he did," I agreed.

"Remember when Tommy was an aviator and everyone jumped out of the plane?" Pablo reminisced.

"Yes, and remember when he went on that wonderful tour of the sewage system and made friends with a rat?"

"I don't remember that," Pablo said.

"That was the night we watched Fleetwood Mac on TV and you complained that nobody wrote good dog lyrics any more."

"Did I say that?"

"You sure did. . . . And then we even wrote our own dog song which I happen to have right here between the pages of this dictionary."

"Read it," Pablo said. "It probably stinks."

I read:

A piece of dog nailed to a weed
A dog without a back;
A dog which does not drive;
A (brown) dog without content!

"No one could sing that," Pablo complained, "it doesn't rhyme and it doesn't reason."

"I also wrote a dog essay for you; come on, you remember. I was high and someone was knocking on the door, and I didn't want to answer it, so I wrote till the knocking stopped. Remember?" I kicked Pablo to make him remember.

"Read it," Pablo said. "It's my only love letter."

I stood on a chair and, gesticulating wildly, repeated Pablo's "love" letter which he had heard only once: "Is there any dog on which one can sit, as on a chair? Yes/no. Perhaps there only exists a dog on which one can spit; the utilitarian dog. The dog without any purpose. What we call a dog belongs equally to what we call our spirit as to what we call our body. Let us try to make a dog without feet or tail which would be as good as a complete dog. And a poem is just like a dog. It has its own language and since everything exists only through language, he forms, in spite of his 'turd psychology' which is imposed by other species, the new dog and the craven universe; that is his function. I dedicate this essay to Pablo whom I love."

"Whistle when you want me," Pablo said lyrically. "I'm your salty dog."

7 Don't think I kept Pablo cooped up at all times. He is a champion swimmer. Three times a week after midnight we would sneak into the hotel pool (located in the basement) for some exercise. I would skinny-dip; he of course could not remove his coat, but when he was wet, how his muscles rippled and rerippled.

It was a pretty pool surrounded with Casbah narrow arches, colored tile, and small circular windows high up on the walls. The light was dim and the room suffused with lacteal illumination. Pablo swam in green milk, his eyes blurry from too strong a concentration of chlorine in the water.

Water is not native to me; I sink. My father tried to teach me how to swim: he would put his arms out just below the surface and I would lie there supported, almost floating. When he removed his arms for an instant I went under. For years I have tried to overcome my panic by staying under for short periods of time. Pablo's presence helps me.

Following is a list of things I say to myself in the hopes of becoming a water baby:

THE COSMOPOLITAN GIRL

STAY UNDER WATER
SUPPRESS PANIC
ASSUME FETAL POSITION
FLOAT TO TOP
THERE IS ENOUGH AIR
I WILL NOT DROWN
I AM IN CONTROL
I AM BOUYANT
I CAN EMERGE
I BREATHE
I FLOAT
MY LIMBS ARE FREE
I AM NO LONGER A PUPPET

Repeating this does not free me. Instead I hear water rushing into my ears and nostrils; I see the four paws of Pablo paddling toward me; then his mouth on my arm pulling.

Lying beside the pool I vowed that it was too much of a sacrifice to accompany Pablo to the pool. Just as some people don't dare look down from a height for fear of falling (jumping?), I don't dare go in too deep (the baptism unto death).

8

Last night I went to Daddy's house. It's on Beekman Place. Across the East River is a big PEPSI-COLA sign; it's almost a part of Daddy's art collection because you can see it from his floor-to-ceiling living room windows. He's rich but not generous with me; in fact I hardly share in his good fortune at all. He expects me to work for a living! If it wasn't for his weird gift of healing people with flowering herbs, penetrating gazes, and massive masterly massage he'd be on relief or washing dishes somewhere. There is nothing the man can do besides putter around with the ill health of others. He's almost as rich as one of those Indian maharishis who travel around in gold Cadillacs, or mountain-hop in hand-painted private planes. Daddy is not so blatant. He wears a tieless shirt, baggy black trousers, and a V-necked wool cardigan. I respect him for his lack of style.

Daddy's art collection is nearly all New York school (abstract expressionism) because, he says, the paintings remind him of the well-worn palms of men of experience. He reads the paintings like palms: "There's the lifeline," (a diagonal streak of red cut across by a tipsy wobble of yellow) he explains, "rich, free, but becoming cowardly toward the end. Each brushstroke brings fear of change while actually in flux." De Kooning's devouring monster women remind him of Mother: her ominous oracular self, her flayed being suddenly exposed and laid bare to cutting winds. "Notice the similarity, the shocked expression in the face and the whirlpool eyes revolving madly," he said to me, holding a photo of Mother alongside the De Kooning painting.

Mother is magical. Daddy is magical. They made me . . . ordinary. There is nothing in the future I foresee. No one I am called to heal but myself.

I do love Edward (Daddy's name), but he doubts it: "You only come here to ask for things," he says. "You never show affection. When I call you, you seldom return my calls. How much longer can I go on trying to reach you when you don't respond?"

Why doesn't he know that I can't? I'm different: not one of his patients who relate symptoms. He has always paid more attention to them. They are his career, his inner life, his real family. Each new case presents an opportunity for him to absorb himself in himself, to wander among the flowers of his knowledge: he plucks the right ones, gathers his bouquet, and presents it to an illness . . . not to me. What is his relationship to the sick? Why must he cure? I don't understand it. Healing is only temporary; a stopgap measure before death claims us one way or another. What difference if a stranger sickens and dies sooner?

"You want to be all-powerful," I told Daddy. "You want to duel with death."

"Nobody duels any more," he answered me. "Healing is not a clash of swords, it is a gathering of facts. You know that."

"I'm not speaking of method," I said. "I'm talking to you about your self-image. How do you think of yourself?"

"Do you really want to know, or are you being hostile again?"

"I want to know, Daddy." I kissed his soft hairy cheek. Some spittle from his mouth clung to the edge of my lip. It tasted like rosewater.

"That's a tough question to answer," he responded, finally taking my hand in an affectionate fatherly grasp, "but even as a small boy, any human being, bird, or creature in pain or distress aroused in me such compassion and desire to help their suffering that I determined to be a doctor. I was also a dreamer, and would dream that healing power flowed from my hand to all those I touched. I couldn't stand the noise of cities and had a tendency to visit with nature. Later, I combined the two great interests of my life and found that I was not merely dreaming. I do not feel superior to those I help and I am certainly humble in the face of calamity!"

Daddy gave me a marvelous fresh strawberry mousse and a piece of home-baked fruit-and-brandy cake while he worked on a patient. I was allowed to watch. The man was stretched out in one of the guest bedrooms on the third floor. At first he seemed nervous, jumped at the slightest noise: door chimes, a drawer closing, Beethoven's Seventh. He was sweating copiously (Daddy asked me to pat him dry with soft cloths, which I did as carefully as I could). Then the man lay down again shaken and helpless. He seemed in constant dread of something. I offered him some strawberry mousse but he refused.

"I suffer from flatulence and constipation," he said to me, thinking I was a medical person, too. Daddy hadn't introduced me as his daughter. "And I have a constant backache," he added dolefully. I would have advised him to eat stewed prunes and Grapenuts every morning for breakfast, but Daddy brought in the following remedies which the man eagerly took one after the other: Rock Rose for his terror, Cherry Plum for his fear of doing something desperate. ("I want to hang myself sometimes," he said. "I've had the urge ever since I heard Billie Holiday sing 'Strange Fruit.'")

Daddy spooned elixir of Aspen into the man's mouth for his fear of the unknown, gave him a tiny blue bottle of extract of Mimulus for his fear of people and noises, placed in the man's jacket pocket a box of Sweet Chestnut for his most unbearable mental anguish, set aside a transparent Lucite casket holding Scleranthus, for his unbalanced, uncertain state of mind, and fed him Agrimony for his unrest.

Immediately the man's bowels worked normally, much to his embarrassment. It must have been the aspen, which has been known since antiquity as a remedy against tapeworms, and cleans you out.

Finally I had Daddy alone in the dining room. His guests (daily freeloaders who came to adore Daddy and call him a genius) had already eaten and were wandering around the living room watching the riverboats, the Pepsi sign, and each other. Most of Daddy's friends were young and in an advanced state of inner peace. This tranquility led them to sit on the floor instead of the chairs or couches which were far more comfortable. I was attracted to a pretty man who sat upright: a young fertile stem (magnified) of the marsh horsetail. He had a harmonica in his mouth which he played without hands. The sound of the two chords he blew (the Amen chorus, F major to C major) was a kind of humorous comment on the meditative atmosphere of the room. I decided to take him home with me because (1) I needed a few laughs, and (2) he had a beautiful body.

Daddy got down to basics right away: "Do you have a job yet?" he asked.

"I'm looking," I answered, "but you know, it's got to be glamorous and interesting."

"Which means you are without funds again?"

I idly picked up a piece of carved jade that was sitting on a shelf behind me and put it in my pocket. Daddy would never miss it.

"All I need is fifty dollars to tide me over," I said. "Come on, love, give it to me."

"Tide you over? You know what happens to rocks when the tide rolls over them? They become sand, a vast indistinguishable beach washed out to sea or packed together into mute bulwarks."

I felt the mute but valuable bulwark in my pocket. It would suffice if Edward was having one of his stingy days.

"For Christ's sake, Daddy, don't wax poetic on me, or I'll tell the world you're a selfish rat. You really are you know."

Daddy pounded the table in anger. "Get a hold on yourself. What happens when the money I give you runs out?"

"When the tide runs out, treasures are left behind," I said.

"Shipwrecks are left behind!" Daddy insisted. Whenever he saw me he saw disaster.

"Please, Dad, look at how skinny I am. Pablo says I'm too thin."

"Pablo?"

"The man I'm living with, you oughtta meet him."

"Really? Why?"

"He's a kick, you'd love him. We do an animal act together. He used to be in vaudeville and small circuses." I could see that Daddy didn't believe me. He turned away and wiped his hand across his eyes as if shielding himself from an awful sight. That awful sight was me.

"Describe your act," Daddy challenged. "You couldn't make less in show business than you're making now. Maybe it's an inspired choice."

"Well," I hesitated, trying to remember any animal acts I had ever seen. "What I do is . . . I am dressed in a sexy leotard with sheer tights and my feet are enhanced by a pair of high-heeled boots. In my hands I hold a hoop. Beyond the hoop is a plain kitchen table. The dog waits for my command. 'Jump!' I say as sternly as I can. 'Jump through the hoop!' But the dog doesn't budge. I say: 'Now, jump up on the table!' But the dog doesn't budge. He doesn't do anything I ask him to. The audience breaks up. Disobedience is the backbone of my act. Isn't it a wonderful idea? Can't get bookings though. Agents are looking for conformity."

"Haven't I seen that act on television recently?" Daddy guessed. How was I to know that he too could be distracted by the luminous boob tube?

"Yes," I admitted. "Wasn't it wonderful?"

Daddy changed the subject, unwilling to discuss the merits of a dog act with me. "How's your mother?" he asked.

"Fine. Still overpaying her help."

"You mean Albert?"

"Who else? He's the only lover she's got. I guess he really answers her needs as well as the telephone."

"And I supposed I don't?" Daddy fumed.

"But Edward, you and Mommy haven't been together for five years. Whatever are you talking about?"

"There is more to life than the physical. We have other ways of communing."

"Glad to hear that," I said. And then: "Goodbye."

"You're not leaving without your money?" Edward asked.

"Oh, am I getting it?" I feigned surprise. This was our little game. Edward would never let me get out of there penniless. He'd then have to worry about whether I was dying of starvation. The publicity would be bad for his reputation. He went to his green metal cashbox, took out exactly fifty dollars, and handed it to me. Taking his money was the thin thread that bound us. If I didn't bounce around too much, it would never break.

The young man with the long hair and mournful harmonica came home with me.

9

"Hello, we're here," I called to Pablo as I opened the door. He was lying glumly in front of the TV watching a game show.

"None of the prizes interest me," Pablo said. "What would I do with a set of power tools?"

"Pablo, this is Reggie, a friend of Dad's. I've told him all about you."

"Hi," Reggie said, getting down into a deep knee-bend, closer to Pablo. "Helen told me you're into sports."

"I play ball," Pablo answered, "and also run track, wrestle, swim . . . you name it." He was warming up to Reggie. "What I really like to do is fetch and carry."

"Not exactly an Olympic event," Reggie said good-naturedly. "Wanna hear a blues tune?" He played a blues thing, this time cupping the instrument in his hands. Pablo got up and danced. It was just like a party.

"You guys thirsty?" I brought out a bottle of beer and some milk. Pablo loves milk. Reggie sprawled on the floor drinking his beer. I got into something comfortable and sheer. "Tell me about yourself," I said to Reggie. "Tell me what you want outta life." This got him started on a lot of talk I didn't understand at all. Stuff about sports averages.

"There are a lot of things I can do that I

haven't done yet. Until I do them I'm shortchanging myself."

"Like what?" I asked.

"I've never batted .300 or hit 50 home runs in a season. I haven't won two MVP awards or played on three world championship teams."

"Why would you want to?" I asked, a trifle unsympathetically. "You can't be into peace, healing, harmonicas, and sports at the same time . . . can you?"

"I can do anything I put my mind to," Reggie said. "I've been approached for a three-year contract, but it would have to be in the vicinity of three million dollars. . . . I'm not going to sell myself cheap."

"Three million dollars is cheap for what you have to offer," I exclaimed, thinking he was playing some game I hadn't got the hang of yet. Reggie didn't seem to be spaced out. His voice had the ring of authority (yet who but madmen are that sure of themselves?). "Can I manage you?" I said, kissing the back of his neck. He smelled peppery, a combination of Patchouli and Holy Smoke.

"You can open another beer for me," he replied, then belched. "My compliments to the chef."

I was so glad I had bought giant, soft pillows to strew around. A good-looking man was just what I had imagined lying on them. I put the icy wet can of beer beside Reggie, and began to unbutton his shirt.

"I aim to fulfill my talents, play up to the peak of my ability," he said, taking my hand and placing it seductively over his crotch.

"How did you meet my father?" I asked, leaving my hand where he had put it. His penis began to rise, elevating my hand ever so slightly. I could feel his sex heat steaming through his trousers.

"I had trouble with my arm, couldn't move it. Had gone to all kinds of doctors. Mother knew about your father's gift for healing so she brought me to him . . . and look . . . nothing's wrong with me now." His hand swept in a full arc, his elbow bent and unbent, he lifted the can of beer and gulped it down. Pablo brought Reggie his chewed-up old tennis ball, and ignoring me, they began to play. I waited my turn (for the turn of the screw), because that's what we did after Pablo trotted to a shadowy corner and took a snooze.

"Are you clean and free of disease?" I asked Reggie, trying to make the question sound cute.

"You can always trust an athlete," he answered.

10 How to tell Pablo that I got the clap from Reggie? It was a mistake. I've always been very careful; however, I must have been receptive to the disease-carrying organism. Now I'm itchy and have a discharge. I know better than to be ashamed; the doctor'll give me a double shot of penicillin to cure it.

11 Pablo has taken the news rather well. There is only a hole in the blanket to show how upset he was, and a few stray hairs which he shed instead of tears.

"Chairman Mao has the right idea," Pablo said. "Venereal disease is practically nil in Red China. The Mao government has almost succeeded in eliminating extramarital sexual intercourse."

"What an unsympathetic thing to say to me," I complained. "Besides, how do you know?"

"I heard it in the elevator," Pablo answered, "from a recent guest of the All-China Medical Association."

12 I've been worried about what will happen to Pablo in his old age and so, projecting into the future, I wrote a letter to Dr. Foster, who gives advice to animal owners. He has always been kind and considerate to those who write in.

Dear Dr. Foster:
I raised Pablo from a young pup. That was when his mother rejected him. He's been my baby since, you might say. A year ago the nineteenth of this month, he turned completely blind and everybody started telling me to get rid of him because he was too old. I haven't seen one friend since I told her I'd rather have her put to sleep than my dog. Of course, Pablo is still with me and always will be. Why does everyone keep saying how old he is? Pablo is only a teen-ager.

H.J.

Dear H.J.:
Understandably, some people are not even able to contemplate giving up a beloved pet. Pablo has been so close to you all these years, the thought of not always having him may simply be unacceptable. Certainly, the fact that a dog is blind does not mean that he cannot enjoy life. I have known many blind dogs who went about the process of living with great gusto. But aging is a process that cannot be denied in any species. Most dogs don't make it to the teens at all. Those who do succumb to various aging processes in the early teens. I am sure with the help of your veterinarian you are doing all you can for Pablo to bring him along as far and as comfortably as possible. But your teen-ager's

time cannot be extended indefinitely by modern medicine, or even by love.

DR. FOSTER

13 I hold in my hand a newspaper clipping that refers to Pablo's short-lived career as a juvenile delinquent. This is the way he came into my life.

PUPPY TELLS GUILT

DOG BURGLAR SEIZED
AFTER 21 BREAK-INS

SCARSDALE.—A New York puppy has admitted breaking into 21 homes, police said Thursday. The dog burst into howls when confronted by police. "It breaks my heart," said Det. Phil Saunders, indicating his chest. The dog committed the burglaries during the last six weeks. First he took only food, an old slipper, and a blond wig, but he became more sophisticated after older dogs told him he was wasting his time with minor loot. He then took watches, jewelry, and portable radios which he left at hock shops on the Lower East Side—his haul amounting to $300–$400 in each one, police said. "He knew it was wrong," said Saunders. "It was because he wanted things. It's a want type of situation." The mode of operation used by the young pup was to scrape with his paw on doors in the neighborhood to see if anyone was home, police said. If no one answered, he would find an open window, push in the screen, and climb inside. He would leave the same way. Saunders suspected from the start that a small creature was involved because of the small windows he climbed through and the nature of the losses. He caught the dog after a routine follow-up of a house burglary. Saunders questioned neighbors who reported seeing a small dog (part collie, part police). They said they had caught the same dog trying to break into their home but had not reported the incident because it was a dog. Saunders went to the pet store where the dog had lived with his maternal grandmother and seven other dogs to whom he is related. "I asked him if he knew why we were there," said Saunders. "He said, 'Yes, because you want to adopt me,' and started to cry." He said most of the dog's profit apparently was spent for ice cream and hot dogs to give to kids. He was a lonely dog and badly needed a good home. The dog's grandmother said the puppy often would be gone as early as 5 A.M., but would never say where he had been. His parents are separated and apparently live somewhere in Scarsdale. "He might have been searching for them," Saunders said. Saunders recommended counseling for the dog and police said he would not be taken to the pound. Meanwhile, if you have a home and a place in your heart for a dog in need, call LU 9-2222.

I immediately called, and took Pablo in. We have an unspoken pact never to mention it again.

14 Late at night I heard someone stop outside the door. As quietly as I could, I looked through the peephole. There was another eye pressed to the glass. It couldn't see me, but I saw it. The iris was hazel with a ring of blue. A beautiful eye. Was it the eye of someone who wants to harm me?

15 Beware of the dog, it bites!

16 I know that Pablo has been sending letters to magazines and newspapers ever since I taught him to type. The roll of stamps becomes narrower and narrower. There are only five stamps left. I found the carbon of a letter he sent to a sex magazine. It amuses him to pretend that he is human, or is he making fun of us? Anyway, I think it's perfectly awful of him to leave the evidence (obscenity) around.

Dear Editor:

Both my wife and I are grateful to S.M. whose frank letter we read with great interest in your September issue. We are carnivores, with some curiosity in whole grains, and so the information intrigued us even more. Having been married for fifteen years, I must admit to you that sexual intercourse was becoming rather infrequent, and when it did take place, rather dull. Then, happily, in your publication came the first intimation of new joys!

The initial time I tried eating medium-sized milk bones from the immaculate vessel of my wife it did not work; milk bones absorb moisture at an alarming rate, and that's the way the cookie crumbled. Next I tried a well-trimmed club steak; this worked marvelously well. By the time I had reached the last bite my wife was perilously close to orgasm. Knowing enough to keep rolling when the dice are hot, we went on to all manner of delights: chopped sirloin, which

I removed morsel by morsel with a pair of ivory chopsticks, old-fashioned Wheatena prepared ahead of time then fried within the "natural female oven" (the rough grain gave us both a gorgeous tingle). Obviously a jaded palate would not appreciate this simple fare, but we deemed it a pleasure to take our breakfast, lunch, and dinner in bed.

Keep publishing your informative, truly adult magazine.

Yours truly,
Pablo Andalou D.O.G.

17 "You haven't told me what you think about the letter you found," Pablo said.

"I think it's quite unusual," I answered without enthusiasm.

"I wrote it to amuse you. You never smile any more." He stood by nervously, hoping I'd thank him or at least scratch his back for him.

"Don't you ever get tired of trying to make me happy?" I said unkindly.

Pablo leaned both front paws on the window-sill. "You don't know how tired," he answered.

18 This evening when I went to the store for juice someone followed me. When I turned around he ducked into a doorway. If he continued following me I would have blown the whistle on my key chain. The advertisement said that the whistle is guaranteed to bring help immediately. I'm glad that I didn't have to blow it.

19 We had to get out of the city, so Pablo and I planned a picnic. "It must be at a fairly deserted place," Pablo said, "so that we won't be bothered." I chose a cemetery in Queens. Pablo carried the blanket and I the bag lunch. The man at the gatehouse assumed we were going to picnic on our own prepaid plot. He did not notice that Pablo was a dog. So many men wear beards and moustaches these days, and besides, Pablo had the brim of his hat pulled down over his ears. Though this made his ears damp he didn't complain.

The parklike flavor of the cemetery and its relative seclusion made it a perfect place for us to visit. Other cemeteries permit ice skating on ponds or encourage strollers; some even substitute see-through fences for their tall stone walls. But this memorial park was old-fashioned enough to retain its stone walls and also its marble monuments instead of indulging in the current trend to bronze lawn-level markers (which reduces the cost of mowing the grass).

"It's been a long time, perhaps a year, since I've come here," I said to Pablo.

"Pardon me, but you've never been here," Pablo said. "At least you've never mentioned it before."

"That's true, but I thought it would be a proper thing to say. Actually I've never been to any cemetery, they scare me."

"Then eat this ham sandwich with cole slaw and mustard. It'll make you feel better."

Pablo plied me with food, and it did make me feel happy and brave and alive. "I think we should know everything about each other," I said confidently. "While there is still time."

"That's not possible," Pablo replied. "I'd rather we rolled in the grass together. I love rolling in the grass. It's so aphrodisiac."

"Anything is possible when you're young and in love," I retorted. "Here we are, just the two of us . . . let's open our hearts to one another."

Pablo opened his mouth. He breathed in short fast takes, gasping doggy fashion. His tongue hung out impolitely; the dull reddish-black papules that normally line the underside of a dog's tongue resembled soft vestigial teeth—his real teeth (fangs) extended past the upper part of his mouth, reminding me of stiffened corn tassels.

"Okay, I'll tell you about myself," Pablo agreed. "These are the scientific facts. I carry, in every drop of my blood, chemical proof of a close relationship to wolves, foxes, and jackals of every species. Although hundreds of thousands of years have elapsed since my direct ancestors lived, and though there has been no blending of blood in the intervening centuries, something rich and brutal has been transmitted." He looked at me hoping that his information would terrify me and thus bolster his male ego, but I remained unperturbed.

"Just what are you getting at?" I asked.

Pablo showed me the newspaper clipping he had been wearing in his hatband for decoration.

HUNT RAPIST WITH FANGS

LINDENHURST, QUEENS, *Aug. 22* (AP)—Police combed shopping marts and parks near this quiet community today for a man with fanglike teeth who raped a middle-aged woman.

The man leaped out of some bushes naked and attacked the woman as she was feeding pigeons, police reported.

The woman said her long-haired assailant appeared to be uneducated, since he did nothing but growl and otherwise utter unintelligible sounds. Police have checked three mental institutions in the area, but so far no inmates have been reported missing.

I was incredulous. "Don't tell me that was you!"

Pablo had that finky cement-set smile mooning his face. "I just want you to realize that I'm not Mr. Nice Guy," he said.

"Oh go chase a bird. That's your speed."

We spent the rest of the time chasing each other: hiding behind tombstones, falling, rising, shouting, and singing at the top of our lungs. We were careful to clean up after ourselves. We wanted to come back and could not afford to antagonize the watchman.

20

Just because Pablo and I have a platonic relationship doesn't mean that I don't dream of a passionate embrace that would weld us even closer together. We have so much in common: a fear of mysteriously moving shadows, avoidance of strangers, intolerance of hot or cold climates, a fearsome hate for being yanked along against our will. But is that enough?

21

"Sorry to bother you again so soon, Mother, but I need some advice."

Mother was wearing her long black robe with hidden pockets. She fumbled around in its folds till she found her steel-rimmed granny glasses and put them on. I observed her coldly, devoid of affection. Every time I saw her I tried to crush the tiny capsule of devotion that was choking me. Why couldn't I experience her as just another human being? She had none of the beauty left that had caused Daddy to compare her to a garden flower. Perhaps he had been thinking of her secret parts when he called her "my very own bearded iris." Mother, afraid of an emotional showdown, kept her professional distance, always.

"Have you come for a private consultation?" she asked.

"Yes. Do you have the time?" I responded coldly.

"I can give you an hour," she replied.

"Thank you, Mother."

"There is a larger fee for the private consultation," she added.

"I'll be able to pay you. Daddy gave me some money."

"Oh? How is your father?"

"He says he's in communication with you, so you ought to know how he is."

"Your father is imagining things."

"I think he wants to get together with you again, Mom."

"That is impossible," she intoned. "I could never live in a household that rang with the cries of those in pain. Edward seems to thrive on it. You know I must have the relative peace of the world of the dead, spirits who materialize only to calm the living or to set them on the right path. Besides, you know I'm living with Albert!" Her voice rose to a fiery pitch. "Albert is the only person who may tap my center of accumulated energy. Your father had his chance!"

Suddenly calm, Mother motioned for me to sit opposite her. Between us, on a round table two feet in diameter, stolidly sat a crystal ball (the future's transparent gossipmonger). I had been with Mother when she had bought the ball at a discount. Its crystal was imperfect, full of bubbles and flecks of color. Mother adored it because it was "different"; she expected it to increase her psychic powers. Gazing into the crystal, Mother said: "Helen Jones, I am receptive to your spirit this evening. It shines with unwavering brightness and tells me that now . . . now is the time for you to forge ahead with financial plans for the future. If you apply for a job tomorrow, you will have great success. Do not hesitate. You have nothing to lose but the double fare. Friends made during the next week will prove beneficial to you, if, and I emphasize the IF, if you do not allow them to walk all over you the way you have in the past. Do not refuse an unusual invitation, and remember that experience is the best teacher, and that life is not a correspondence course. If you have any questions, ask them now, before the vision fades away."

"Reverend Jones," I began, hoping that Mother would not fly into a rage when I asked my question, "why did you and Daddy separate?"

Mother removed her steel-rimmed glasses (which didn't have lenses in them. She only wore them to make her look owl-wise) and tapped them angrily on the table. A sharp pain in my left leg told me that she had kicked me under the table.

"Don't you remember when Edward spread those stories about me? I spit on him!" She shouted to Albert to bring in her private file, then plucked from its accordian-pleated folds a Xeroxed copy of father's ignominious attack which had appeared in the papers.

SAUNA BURNS BASIS
OF DIVORCE ACTION

Burns suffered in an East Side sauna have converted a 36-year-old "devout Prudist," mother of one child, into a loose woman who sips brandy Alexanders in bars and has affairs with strange men, according to an attorney who filed a divorce suit against Mrs. Myra Jones naming the spa as contributing to the corruption of Mrs. Jones's morals.

THE COSMOPOLITAN GIRL

Dr. Edward Jones testified that since his wife, Mrs. Myra Jones, was burned in the sauna two years ago she has become two persons, physically and psychologically speaking. As *Myra* Jones she exerts great sexual powers over younger men from whom she receives money, much of which is spent on the brandy Alexanders, which she craves. But as *Mrs. E.* Jones she remains the "shy" person and devout Prudist she was before she became a victim of the faulty thermostat (which has been replaced) at the Citrus Health Spa.

The doctor described his wife *Myra* Jones as "the sexually hungry production of *Myra*'s mind" and *Mrs. E.* Jones as "the guilt-ridden projection who bitterly regrets her actions." He said that Mrs. Jones has been sexually involved "with at least a dozen other men" since her accident in the sauna. "On one occasion I had to follow her to Mexico to get her away from someone she met in a bar," he said. The doctor claims that now she has developed sex feelings for strangers, and that those feelings often take control when she is sipping brandy while seated near men in a bar. So far, the spa has refused to comment on the charges officially, but employees have been heard to remark off the record that since the publicity, business has picked up considerably.

"How many lies do you count in that article? How many?" Mother insisted.

"At least three," I replied. "You're not devout,

you've never been burned in a sauna, and you don't like brandy. You have been known to associate with strange young men though . . . Albert for one."

"Edward was jealous . . . excessively jealous. I'm not about to give up my strange young strangers, nor the comfortable neighborhood bar. Tell Edward that! No don't tell him. Why stir up dead passions? Your father may be Edward Jones physician and humanitarian to others, but to me he's a seething volcano."

"I think you're both crazy, Mom."

"Thank you, darling," she replied, laughing. "I think we both are too. Now remember, when you go home, to set your clock early for tomorrow. A new and exciting life waits for you."

The Reverend Jones had no reason to believe I would take her motherly advice. I never have.

22

"You've got to level with me, Pablo; I can't find my gold pants and jacket. . . ."

"You can't?"

"No, I can't. And I haven't even worn them yet. Remember that package I received from the Mistress Collection by Funky?"

"No."

"Look here, Mr. Innocent, something very weird is happening; my favorite clothes have been disappearing."

"I'll help you look for them if that's what you want."

"I've already looked everywhere."

"Clothes just don't get up and walk out by themselves, do they?"

"Pablo, do you know something you're not telling me?"

"No."

23 Mother did not meet Albert at a séance. She met him as he roamed a local hospital's halls wearing a white jacket and a stethoscope that he had bought at Sears with a fraudulent credit card. Police had been looking for a phony doctor who'd plied unwary widows with expensive gifts in order to "take them for all they've got," Mother told me. She admired his many successful impersonations of those in respected professions: the lawyer, the surgeon, the banker, and the scientist. In spite of a lack of formal schooling, Albert gave advice that was always excellent and based on a cram course of self-initiated study. He could have been eminent in any of the aforementioned fields if he had not been a mental case. Diversity itself is an illness; it bespeaks an uncertain cast of mind. One other thing. Albert adored setting fires, and the charming but dangerous outcast was grateful to Mother for trusting him with the lighting of the chapel candles (in spite of a few regressions) and for shielding him from the law.

She doesn't know that I've been seeing Albert since he first took the folded piece of paper out of my hand. I love intrigue and bugging Mother. Outside of that Albert has no great attraction for me. It's a game. But who knows?

24 Albert deserves a physical description, since that is what is most elusive about him. Once he is fixed firmly in my mind, none of his disguises can confuse me.

HAIR: Brown, with a preponderance of red highlighting each pomaded wave

EYES: Green, planted at uniform dept within a narrow furrow

NOSE: Stuffed toucan

MOUTH: Sensitive, twitching

TEMPERATURE: Warm to the touch like a low-wattage bulb

HABITS: Scratches behind the ear till it bleeds

RULES: Will not tie his shoelaces in public. Will not live within ten miles of the maddening stillness of the Negev

FAMILY: He is the son of a well-known hermaphrodite who managed to impregnate himself/herself after receiving the medical opinion that it was an impossibility. Such is the ingenious stuff that Albert is made of

FEAR: That he will one day throw the wheat away with the chaff

25

Albert called. He was coming over. I knew I looked a mess, and so his call sent me into a flurry of activity. How could I believe I was beautiful unless I saw myself through his eyes? Unless I made *sure* he'd go ape over me. I turned to my longtime friend and adviser *Cosmopolitan* magazine. "Oh *Cosmo*," I pleaded, "how can I look superstunning on short notice? Help me!" As if by chance, I came upon these words: "BEAUTY HINTS. YOUR ZIP-ZAP SPLIT-SECOND ROUTINE. GUARANTEED TO PERFORM MIRACLES." Just what I needed . . . a miracle. I followed *Cosmo*'s suggestions to a T: first I stripped down to the mere essentials, naked as the day I was born, although Mother told me I was wearing a blood-red chemise molded from hot wax when I first appeared between her legs. Then I stretched and pulled my body as if blocking a wet curtain. Next I washed my face and applied egg white and lemon juice, letting it dry to become a thin *masque*. When the *masque* hardened, it was as if I were removing my face. I had in my hands an incomplete, compacted death mask. Because of the lack of time, I whipped out a dry shampoo for my not-quite-clean hair, and then took the risk of falling asleep beneath eye pads soaked in witch hazel and ice water. While I lay there I thought only beautiful thoughts, since distressing ruminations on life and death are *taboo* if you want to be beautiful. I thought of being out in the open with Daddy, of transplanting young plants who could not in some cases extend their roots fast enough to keep up with the gradually disappearing moisture of boxes set in greenhouses. I breathed rhythmically through my nostrils, which was necessary for more happy brain waves. Because I have always considered feet to be desperately important, I hopped into the tub and let blasts of hot and cold water beat against my soles. It felt so good I wondered what I needed Albert for? The soles of my feet are as sensitive as my nipples (what an inelegant location for an erogenous zone!). After drying and perfuming my feet I put on my cuddlyest slippers and became a speed demon . . . but not slapdash. I knew that Albert would view me with close scrutiny; he was extremely nearsighted, and what he couldn't see he could smell. He reminded me of Pablo in that respect. But what of my face? Yes, I do wear makeup sometimes: for cheeks a peach blush-on bronzing gel; for fabulously murky eyes my favorite color is sad shadow and gobs of old-fashioned black salve (you can get it at the drugstore and it also draws pus out of wounds and pimples); my lips are painted cherry red, but for that neglected area between the upper lip and tip of nose I brush just a teensy-weensy suggestion of a moustache. Albert adores moustaches, he's bi-hirsute. I knew he would respect me for my political statement regarding androgeny as it reposed in my moustache. He did not regard hairiness as being unfeminine; in fact he carried about with him a photograph of a Turkish woman whose face rivaled that of Grace McDaniel's, who was once billed as THE UGLIEST WOMAN. Almost ready for Albert, I jolted my senses with a splash of cologne and put perfume behind my ears and on all pulse points. With thirty seconds to spare I sat down to wait for Mother's protégé.

26

I did not have intercourse with Albert. I was too beautiful and clean. It would have taken hours for me to repossess my naturalness. Besides, Albert was wearing a disguise that put me off; he had come as Gertrude Stein. Aside from the necrophiliac tendencies it might have revealed in me if I had balled Albert cum Stein, I did not want to discover that yes, Gertrude did have a penis, which is why she hid herself beneath such voluminous skirts of fat.

"In profile I look like an Indian," Albert said. "Stein's greasepaint is fabulous."

Haughtily turning, he waited for me to agree.

"Maybe you do," I said, "but what's the point?"

Albert was disappointed in me. "There isn't any point. It's just an experiment. I love to dress up and be different."

"You don't talk different. You talk like Albert."

"No, no, I talk like Gertrude Stein. Yesterday the Reverend Jones drew her into our circle. I studied her articulation, the things she said. I . . ."

He gurgled deep down in his throat, took a few staggering steps backward, clutched at his jacket lapels, and continued in a voice that was deeper and yet ephemeral. It might have come from that place between heaven and hell; it might have traveled down from the eighteenth floor. It was a ghostlike voice. As the words emerged, Albert mimicked a striptease.

"I am loving, when I am loving I am saying I am loving. Yesterday I was not loving. Not loving is not loving any day. Today is a day I am loving. Today is here. Loving and today are words. All words do not say I am loving. What is loving when one is not feeling that one is loving? . . ."

"Hate?" I innocently asked. Albert was too far gone to answer me.

"Alice, *à quelle heure sont Ernest et Pablo* arriving? Does the fish smell? Have you ironed my manuscripts? Chocolates are for saints. No, I won't go, I've changed my mind. My, my, how firm the carrots are. I'm the only genius who knows who all the other geniuses are! Our trip to America will be triumphant, *un succès d'estime.* Don't worry, our relationship is ambiguous only to the underprivileged. *Au revoir et à bientôt, ma cherie."*

He aurevoired himself right into the bathroom, where he recovered after drinking a small bottle of paregoric which I had been keeping for toothache.

"Feel better?"

"Much."

"You look better without your makeup and skirt."

"Thanks."

"What time is it, Albert?"

"Don't know. My timepiece and my codpiece don't work. Overwound I guess."

"It must be late."

"You want me to go?"

"Umhum."

"Do I deserve an Academy Award for my performance this evening?"

"Umhum."

"Thank you. May I see you again sometime?"

"Umhum."

27 I have a collection of poems that men gave me for one reason or another. Sometimes it was to take the place of a gift, or to prove how much they trusted me with their innermost thoughts. Usually it was to prove that they were either sane or totally insane. Conniving romanticists all. The poems were mostly old-fashioned, none of them read like laundry lists, and none of them swarmed across the page like a flight of doves. Flattering but dull. Albert's autobiographical poem was the last in my collection:

MUTABLE MOTHER

I keep thinking of fires we used to make
in the empty lot across the street
littered with garbage where horseflies streaked

THE COSMOPOLITAN GIRL

I was 10, you were old
wild bitter mom, my boyish body
trying over the moist
shadow-mottled girth
no one warned me to stay away from there
Later a fire swept through
the venetian blinds
of our oedipal castle
we blackened
Is the child with shred
of flesh between his legs
still burning?

 People cannot be dealt with like a
disease.

29 My favorite morning program is the
Joe Fafka program. Joe carries on a dialogue with
his listeners. The morons call in, and people like
me just listen and laugh.

CALLER: "Say Joe, just when did this crime wave
start? I think that it was the Kennedy adminis-

tration, with them Young Lords and them
Black Panthers; rotten gripers!
JOE: No, it really commenced with Lyndon B.
Johnson, that big Texas blowhard, when he
said in his drawl: "You have to have your civil
rights!" You see, sir, any time you appease a
tyrant, it only whets his appetite more. He gave
them the go-ahead, and we have to pay for it.
I say starve the scum. Drive them out. Don't
feed and clothe them. Is that what we're pay-
ing taxes for?"
CALLER: Can I say one more thing, Joe?
JOE: You're on.
CALLER: About the Jews in the Middle East . . .
JOE: Get off the phone, you creep!

Joe is wonderful when he's mad, an authentic
bigot.

30 Midmorning and it was Albert's voice
on the phone. A marriage proposal. He said that I
not only reminded him of my mother, but of his
mother, and that I would make him the happiest
man in the world if I consented to be his bride.
Nope," I said.

31

Mother pulled a switch on me. She tried to convince me to marry Albert: "He may be a pyromaniac, but he's not an arsonist!" she shouted. "He does it for love, not money. Don't you want to be loved and adored by a husband and dance the carioca? I'd marry Albert myself, but he's too old for me."

"Mother, nobody's danced the carioca in years," I protested.

"One more word out of you and I'll hang up," Mother warned. "Why don't you fly down to Rio and see for yourself? It's a wonderful place to honeymoon."

"I don't love Albert," I said.

"Neither do I," she said. "I love your father."

So, Mother would sacrifice me, in order to pave the way for a reconciliation with Edward!

"You're not good enough to shine his shoes for him," I retorted angrily.

Mother hung up.

32

I went to a professional for advice, as I always do. Dear Mary answered me in her syndicated column.

ROSALYN DREXLER

Dear Mary:

I suppose to some my problem may seem funny, but to me it's no joke. I've been dating this terrific guy for a few weeks now and we get along great even though I'm taller than he is. He takes me to the best places, and he's a perfect gentleman, but the problem is this, he gets a sexual thrill out of setting fires. You may have read about the fires at Melon's Wax Museum in which two exhibits were destroyed: a Chinese Temple and a representation of the Last Supper; my friend was a prime suspect. The thing is this, should I drop this suitor (he was bequeathed $100,-000,000 in trust from which he is allowed to draw $100,000 a year) or should I continue the relationship?

Sincerely,
Once Burned

Dear Once Burned:

Ask him point-blank if he means to marry you or whether he is just carrying a torch. If he is serious, have him agree on a date. Once married, I suggest you tip off the proper authorities, and hotfoot it away with the loot.

33
There is a madman at large who is fixated on me. This note was slipped under the door.

DON'T THINK YOU
HIDE FRUM ME, I KNOW YOU
CUNT-TITS WHAT LAUGH AT ME
WHEN I WANT TO,
BUT,
I KNOW WHERE SUCK AND FUCK AND,
PUT THE BIG-
GEST COCK IN! ! ! ! ! ! !
I BE FRIEND SOON
SINCERELYELY

34
Because I was upset, Pablo read to me. "Florida. A group of students who had been drinking beer on Dorado Beach visited the Corry Brothers International Circus. They were wandering among the animal cages stored behind the tents, when one of the students broke away from his friends, shouting: 'I'm stronger than you are; let's fight!' He then jumped into the tiger's cage and pulled the tiger's whiskers. The tiger broke his neck with one swipe of its paw."

ROSALYN DREXLER

The item cheered me up enough so that I could jot down these questions. They may lead to a deeper understanding of the inexplicable.

QUESTIONS

1: Why was the tiger wearing false whiskers?
2: Why do students shout when they are together?
3: Why was the tiger's cage open?
4: What did the student learn?
5: Did the jungle beast resemble someone in the boy's family?
6: Was an honorary diploma awarded the boy and placed in the casket beside him?
7: Is it best to live in the cage or out of it?

35 My friend Marian hasn't seen or heard from me since she moved out of the Buckminster. We've been through a lot together and still feel close, but the burden of friendship is on me. Marian lives in a shithole on the Lower East Side with a guy who practically scraped her off the sidewalk when she was already pregnant with Elmer Joy. Marian is a singer and writes her own songs, but since the baby she hasn't had time. Marian is a natural person, and loves to have Elmer Joy at her breast. "It turns me on," she admitted, and look at what it's done for Elmer Joy. True, her kid was fat and healthy. He had come a long way from when he was born prematurely. Marian and Jeremy, Marian's old man, were driving through a snowstorm in Vermont, stopping every now and then to screw (Marian had three more months, she thought, before birth time), when she began to have labor pains. They drove to a local hospital, which happened to have a special unit for premies and newborns with other difficulties, where she gave birth. Elmer Joy had all kinds of tubes in his heart and almost died three times, but the doctor let Marian hold him and nurse him. . . . That, and some infant will to live, pulled Elmer Joy through.

While watching a diaper commercial on TV, I got the impulse to call Marian. I knew it would be an important call and I was right; Marian put me on to a job possibility—selling tacos and soft drinks from a cart. One of her friends was planning to leave, and Marian was sure she'd recommend me.

"But I'd like to see you. Why don't we get together next week, go to the Cloisters or somewhere for a drink?" she said. "I just bought these knockout violet-tinted glasses with pearl frames, you should see them on me, you'll die."

"Okay, so let's meet at your place, say tentatively, next Saturday morning, unless I call you before then," I agreed. "How's Jeremy?"

"He's still on the road with Miracle in Milan, you must have heard of them . . . the new Italian rock band. Jeremy's their road manager. We're doing very well, managed to save ten thousand dollars. Dig it! And we didn't have nothin' when we began."

"Say, that's great! What're you gonna do with all that money?"

"Buy a house in the country, have my own garden. You and Pablo can stay with us whenever you want."

"I love you, Marian."

"I love you, too, Helen."

She gave me her friend's phone number, and her friend said she'd talk to her boss about hiring me when she quit.

36 Pablo and I play Celebrity. It's an interview game we made up. He is usually the journalist, and I am the celebrity.

Pablo with tape recorder going and pencil poised above notebook: "Miss Jones, our readership of young career women between the ages of nineteen and twenty-six would be especially interested in hearing what you have to say to them, since you are one of the most eligible women in the world. . . ."

Miss Helen Jones, seated in front of a huge

picture window: "Yes, I am one of the most eligible women in the world. I speak Greek, Danish, Italian, French, Spanglish, and Tongues. I'm not too old or too poor. I stay stiletto slim by eating only foods that can be prepared with a minimum of fuss. I wear gold chokers around my long white neck. When I make love I allow three elegantly shaped breasts to appear from under my favorite negligee. It isn't difficult for me to keep a year-round pallid complexion since I summer in New York, indoors where the skin-drying sun can't reach me. My playmate and constant companion is Pablo, born a mutt, but a natural aristocrat. He also makes an adequate foot warmer. I don't allow work to interfere with partying in SoHo, Washington Heights, or Little Italy. I feel like Vasco da Gama or Christopher Columbus for having discovered these places. They are sensationally provincial. I used to go to Saint Croix, but since those thirty unexplained murders of whites on the island, I've canceled my reservation. No sense in going where one is not wanted, is there? I own literally thousands of designer dresses which I give away to my favorite charities every two years. I prefer wearing ready-to-wear 'finds' right off the racks. I've already had two well-publicized breakdowns, one at the Forty-second Street library when I tried to feed fifteen pounds of filet mignon to the stone lions, another at Chock Full O' Nuts where I appeared in blackface and roller skates during the lunch hour. Having achieved total peace with my favorite yogi, Meher Barbareebop, who said, *'Don't worry. Be happy. We are all one. I am the ocean of life,'* I no longer need an intelligent, level-headed man to protect me. I practice the kazoo four hours a day and hope to go on concert tours in the near future. I readily admit my humble beginnings on a Georgia dirt farm; in fact I have fond memories of wandering carefree and barefoot through the mud with friends: black, white, pink, or blue. . . . I was already broad-minded. My inquisitive nature lent added pleasure to an otherwise drab childhood. My cigarette is Gauloises. My voice has a husky quality; it went down an octave after I was hit by an overhanging branch while horseback riding. I have no time for a serious romance in my life. I'm never lonely."

Pablo thanked me for the interview and promised to send me a copy of it before it was published, just in case there was anything I wanted to retract. He's not the usual run of journalist.

37 When I mentioned earlier that Marian and I had been through a lot together, one of the things I was referring to was abortion. Last year, in the same week, by means of a vacuum, some pre-

infant material was sucked out of our wombs. Pablo
had been upset because he fancied himself the father
of what might have been. I didn't fancy it at all,
being the mother of wolf-boy, a child with callouses
on elbows and knees, no knack for clear speech, a
reading disability, and complete lack of table man-
ners. The child's name would have reflected our
merger—PabHel Inc.—sure to bring him misery in
school. I was more disturbed over Marian's experience; up till the last minute she hadn't made up her
mind, and then, it was all over. Now, of course, she
has Elmer Joy, and I have my freedom, such as it is.

38 Why work if you don't have to?

39 Cab driver told me to say hello to my-
self every morning, because, "If you don't accept
yourself in a friendly way, no one else will." He also
reminded me that "there ain't no closet small enough
to hold what you need, and no closet big enough to

hold what you want." I tipped him twenty-five cents to the dollar, instead of my usual fifteen cents.

40 Jade is worth three times what it used to be. I can't bring myself to sell the piece I took from Edward; I've grown attached to it. When I look at it I suffer. There is a snail captured in the jade: bluish-green, curled in on itself, and asleep.

41 Another note, this time left in my mailbox behind the desk in the lobby. The clerk said: "I can't remember everybody who comes in." The message was especially vicious. I was not the target, Pablo was. IF WE DON'T GET YOU, WE'LL GET YOUR DOG.

Who are they? What do they want? Pablo is a citizen of the inner city and so am I, both useless to a political plot.

42 Pablo told me of a dream he had in which purebred beagles were pulled out of the trunk of a car in order to be auctioned off, and then taken to laboratories where they were subjected to experiments.

"But you're a mutt," I said to soothe him. "Who would want you?"

"Those who are jealous of our mute partnership, those who are not decent and have lost their faith. Cells of satanic vivisectionists are springing up all over the city. My best friend, Fido, is a good example of the cruelty of these humans. His head was grafted onto the body of another dog. Both heads responded to stimuli, and Fido survived for one terrible month before he died."

"Is that a fact!" I said.

"I didn't just make it up," Pablo answered.

We spent the evening chewing nervously on dog biscuits.

43 I bought postcards of dogs showing them dancing, singing, and beating drums while wearing little pointed hats on their heads. The cards are imported from West Germany.

44 Daddy was beautiful as he went about his laboratory potentizing his flowers by a method he had discovered the year before. "See this little plant, Helen?" he said tenderly. "It grows about a foot in height, is so unassuming that it is easily passed unnoticed. The flowers on its many-branching slender wiry stems are pale mauve in color and very small. They remind me of you as a child."

Taking three small plain glass bowls, he filled them with water and set them under the blue lights that were always lit above his indoor garden. Carefully he placed the flower heads of the chicory plant in one of the bowls till the whole surface of the water was covered. In the second bowl he floated the tiny flowering end sprays of the agrimony, and in the third, those of the vervain (lemony sprigs, delightfully scented).

"In about four hours, when the petals start to fade, the water will be impregnated with magnetic power," Daddy said.

In about four hours the water was crystal clear and full of sparkling bubbles. Daddy lifted the flowers out of the water with a blade of grass so that he would not touch the fluid with his own fingers. The water was then transferred by means of a small-lipped phial to the bottles that were to hold the finished tincture. When the tincture bottles were half full, he added an equal amount of brandy to preserve the fluid and keep it clear indefinitely.

"You'd make a wonderful assistant," Daddy said. "Would you like to learn my methods, help me in my work?"

"Daddy, I'm going on a vacation to Las Vegas, so I can't," I lied, though the minute I said it I became interested in the trip. Decided to ask Albert to go with me. He'd been there before and would be helpful. Mother could finance the excursion; she'd want something in return, of course.

"All your life's a vacation," Daddy said. "You haven't applied yourself to anything. Why are you going to Las Vegas? You don't gamble."

"Curiosity, Dad. The same curiosity you have for plants. I want to play around, find out what happens when one lays a warm poultice of female juice over the palpitating heart of an impotent bystander. I want to extract a dew of the senses from the rigid limbs of those who prefer paralysis to the danger of feeling. I'm my father's daughter."

Edward, obviously moved by my declaration of allegiance, paced the floor of his laboratory. He responded with fatherly scientific persuasion, hoping to get me to give up my disturbing ideas.

"Essences cannot be extracted from people!" he exploded. "Soak a person in a tub and you get a skimming of dead cells. This helps no one; the person in the tub comes out wrinkled as a newborn babe . . . full of torpor. . . ."

"You're not being helpful, Daddy."

"Nobody helped me."

"You didn't need help. You had your passion and the open fields. You went to medical school. You didn't care about clothes and travel. I do!"

"Helen, you are trying my patience! I used to be full of fun; played darts, kept myself fit with boxing, rowed in Central Park lake. In the very early mornings, even on wintry days I would take pleasure in walking in the park by the lake, flinging handfuls of bread crumbs to the hungry ducks or sparrows that landed on the snow. Strangers I met claimed that I awakened in them a renewed sense of joy and interest in life. Because of you I have become somber. You refuse the real gifts I have to offer. You prefer running around without any purpose in life."

"Why don't you try curing me with your flowers?"

"Do you mean it?"

"Yes, Edward, you can treat me."

Edward had never treated a case of filial obstinacy before, so he went through his file and consulted the case history of a woman of thirty-six who had suffered from asthma all her life. She had lost her baby daughter and would sit still for long periods in front of the child's photograph weeping. She seemed to live in a dream, having little interest in the rest of the family.

"You never seem to catch your breath and you

live in a dream," Daddy said. "You have little interest in either myself or your mother except when you come soliciting our help, therefore, your state of mind indicates clematis. After two bottles you should regain your joy in life, and take an interest in your family."

"Thanks, Edward, you're a good dad."

"I expect you to restore my confidence in you," he replied, "and then you won't have to dun me for money, I'll be happy to give it to you."

45 *Cosmo* says: No matter how crassly expressed, the idea behind "Anything goes" is important for our times. Whether your "thing" turns out to be of redeeming social importance is not crucial; it's the *passion* with which you defend your view that's important. And so I've decided to follow my heart by sleeping with my beloved Pablo. What's the difference so long as no one gets hurt? I am woman and Pablo is a consenting adult male . . . dog.

ROSALYN DREXLER

46

MY LIST OF SENSUAL THINGS TO DO BEFORE
SLEEPING WITH PABLO

MY PARAGRAPH OF SENSUAL THINGS I TRIED
BEFORE I SLEPT WITH PABLO

SOME THINGS I TRIED IN ORDER TO BECOME
SEXUALLY AROUSED

I began by blowing soap bubbles but couldn't
get off behind it. I rescued a well-worn pair of jeans,
which a former lover had left at my place, and imagined his super body in them. I crawled over the
floor of my room on hands and knees exploring
every surface, but instead of its making me feel
adventurous and animal-like, I picked up a splinter
in my knee and was furious. I put on a nightgown
and wore it in the shower and got a chill. I went to
an Italian grocery store and smelled all the smells,
but merely got hungry not sexy. I ate sixteen perfect
defrosted raspberries, ate an entire frozen custard
slowly in the dark, studied photos of nude male
statues, and sucked my big toe.

My conclusion was that I should let nature take
its course. If Pablo was destined to drive me wild,
he would, but till then, I would cease and desist ex-
perimenting on myself.

47

Pablo noticed my lack of sleep. Quite truthfully, I told him what I had been trying to do: "I want to sleep with you, but I'm afraid," I said slowly.

"All one has to do is expose one's inner feelings, and fear goes away," Pablo replied.

"That is not easy."

"You spend too much time on ephemerals. Don't worry about what will happen . . . live!"

"You think I should . . . live?"

"Yeah! Listen, Helen, I'm an athlete. I play the game fair, you're on my team, so we're sure to win. Close the lights, shut the door, you don't have to worry any more."

"You're not a very big dog. . . ."

"Big enough."

"We're from different worlds. . . ."

"But we're together now."

"What would my parents say if they knew?"

"What they don't know won't hurt them."

"Do you love me?"

"As much as any slave can love his master."

"Promise you won't come in my mouth."

"No chance of that."

48

Post Coital Message to Pablo

Your fucking is not yet art. One day perhaps you will cry out, stammer incoherently, or grind your teeth together and open your eyes wide, very wide. Fucking is always a matter of the entire personality. For that reason it is fundamentally tragic to mount from the rear and not be able to kiss. Also you did not wash your paws before you had me; there were paw prints around my waist. I am sorry to say that I felt like a dog, uncomplex, the docile receiver of your invading penis. And my eyes were closed (too?) and I was dreaming of a man, no, two men: one lying under me sucking my breasts (Romulus), and one above me (Remus). During a last exertion, you nipped my neck and brought me back to reality. As Johann Wolfgang von Goethe said, "All is struggle, effort. Only those deserve love and life who have to conquer them each day." Isn't that everybody?

49

Pablo has promised to treat me like a person. He will never fuck me again . . . he says. The human smell means nothing to him, and I was too tall, even though I bent over. It embarrassed him and his timing was off. He has a bad knee from trying to hold his position while I skidded forward on the floor.

The first time is never easy, especially with a new species.

50 "Pablo, what have you done with my new sweater?"

"What do you mean?"

"It's missing. I could swear I put it in this drawer."

"Why tell me? I haven't taken it. Your sweaters are far too big for me."

"I haven't accused you, dummy, just thought perhaps you had seen it . . . the white one with sequins around the neck, you said you liked it on me because you could see my nipples through it. Oh, where could it be?"

"Remember when the toilet was stuffed?"

"Yes."

"Maybe it fell down the toilet."

"Maybe it flew out the window and a crowd of moths ate it up."

"Maybe."

"Pablo, I don't think I trust you any more. What have you done with my clothes?"

"Nothing, no-thing, nohohoho-thing.
  Your little doggy's in the clear
  so please don't kick him in the rear
  if of your sweater he does hear
  he'll let you know with all good cheer."

"You don't convince me."

51 Next morning I sulked around. Pablo suggested I listen to Joe Fafka. I had been wanting to discuss the energy crisis with him, the Civil War, and a topic he had brought up briefly a few days before, "What turns you on?" A woman had called and told Joe that his voice turned her on. He informed her that he was appearing at a new supermarket in New Jersey, and that if she was sincere she'd come out to New Jersey to meet him. Another woman, a newlywed, said that it turned her on to greet her husband at the door with no clothes on. I wasn't sure what I'd say if I got through, but impulsively, I dialed Joe's number. I waited fifteen minutes, then someone said, "hello."

"Is this Joe Fafka?" I asked. It didn't sound like him.

"Yes, this is Joe Fafka. Who do you think it is, dummy?"

"Joe?"

"Yes, speaking. You're on the air, ma'am."

"Hello, Joe, I just wanted to tell you and your listeners that people who live in cold rooms live longer, so I don't mind the energy crisis at all and never complain when the heat is turned off. I figure the landlord is doing me a favor."

"Get off the phone, stupid!" Joe yelled. I stayed on. "You're too stupid to know when you're insulted," he continued.

"I know you don't mean it, Joe," I said.

"I do mean it, ma'am. Don't you realize that old people, sick people, and little children are suffering because of lack of heat?"

"Sure . . . but—"

"Well, then, get off the phone!"

"Look, Joe, I want to ask you something else. It's about my boyfriend. We've had premarital sex and now he doesn't want to marry me. What should I do?"

"Kill yourself."

"Really Joe?"

"That is my considered opinion, ma'am."

"One more thing, Joe. I forgot to mention that my boyfriend is a Gemini, born May twenty-second at one A.M. Do you have a feeling about him? What's he really like?"

"Your friend is a typical Gemini—creative but

can't sustain one occupation. He is so excitable that he leaps from one idea to the next. He's never satisfied. He likes to move. Can't stand being in one .place too long. Gemini is adventurous, will try anything once. I get the feeling that your boyfriend has a wet nose. Does he have a cold?"

"No, his nose is always wet, and he scratches a lot but he doesn't have fleas."

"You're pulling my leg, ma'am; thank you for your call and don't call me again. . . ."

"Joe, don't go. . . . I wanted to tell you what turns me on."

"I'll bite. Go ahead, tell your idol Joe Fafka what turns you on, ma'am."

"Your opinions on the Civil War . . . they were so . . . so . . . divergent."

"Anything in particular that I said?"

"Well, I got excited when you talked about how the North used to milk the South by tariff, and how the South bore the ban of slavery while the North got the money for bringing the slaves down south, and how the North bought the cotton, got rich while the South grew poor."

"*That* excites you, ma'am? You're sick. Emotionally ill. Are you calling perhaps from one of our state institutions? I thought I heard a Southern drawl when you opened your mouth. Could you be one of those detestable jungle bunnies; a commie, black, no goodnick on welfare? And why do you call *me* to ask *me* all kinds of questions? I'm not God."

| 87

"You wanna know what you are, Joe? You're an evil, white supremacist bigot!"

With that, the station operator broke our connection, but I turned up the radio to hear Joe say, ". . . coward . . . stupid low life! . . . Now friends, if you have something to celebrate, if you want to take the family out for a truly excellent dinner . . ."

52 At 3 A.M. I heard loud knocking on my door. When I opened it, I found no one. There was a melted puddle of ice in the hall beside the door, and hanging on the doorknob was a skinny, yellow old chicken leg. Since when has Chicken Delight taken up voodoo?

53 Las Vegas here I come! Albert arrived at my door with an overnight bag and a raincoat thrown over his arm.

"Your mother tried to get it out of me but I wouldn't tell her where I was going, or with who," he said breathlessly.

"Don't be silly. Mother knows everything, Albert; she wants you to go with me. Honest!"

"No, Helen, you're wrong. The Reverend Jones is ambivalent, like all women. She doesn't know what she wants."

"Bullcrap!"

Albert began sniveling. "The world isn't safe for young lovers."

I took his bag, shoved him inside, and shocked him with the news that Pablo (whom he hadn't met before) was going with us.

"Pablo?"

"My dog . . . what are you staring at?"

Pablo was walking around on his hind legs, a highball in one paw. . . . He also had an erection.

"Is that Pablo?" Albert asked in consternation. "But I haven't made a reservation for three!"

"That's okay, he can sleep on the floor or at the foot of the bed. Don't worry. He's just a dog."

"I'm just a dog," Pablo repeated. "Look, no opposable thumb."

Albert was forced to examine Pablo's softly clenched paw. "My God, he looks like a dog, but he acts human, and he talks!"

"Mere illusion, he's a trained dog."

"What else does he do?" Albert asked suspiciously.

"He can jump through a hoop of fire."

Albert became visibly excited, his voice took on

an exuberance it had lacked on his arrival. "Hoop of fire? I'd like to see that!"

"You will, in Las Vegas," I promised. "That's why Pablo is coming with us. He's more fun than a barrel of monkeys."

Patting Pablo's head, Albert looked at me and said, "The dog's a treasure. I can understand why you wouldn't want to be away from him for a second."

54

Before we left for the airport, Pablo communicated his hierarchy of rank within our small group. I was the disputed piece of ground, Albert the lower-ranking enemy. Pablo stood erect, body in a normal position, back flat, tail behind him. Albert, submissive, abject creature that he was, wriggled across the room in a crouching walk, his head down, and ears back. Pablo said: "I am top dog, and don't you ever forget it!" The game amused Albert. It had never occurred to him before to obey a dog.

And Mother called, with one of her terrible predictions. She was jealous of me. She wanted all the men in the world for herself. No wonder I can only relate meaningfully to a dog!

"Believe me, Helen, if you go tourist class, three abreast, there will be a disruptive influence seated between Albert and yourself. This disruptive influence has a tendency to become ill during flight. He is a satanic messenger carrying dangerous flatulence which he plans to explode halfway between embarkation point and destination. He will demand an extravagant sum of filet mignon after commandeering the plane. Both you and Albert will become hostages. When you land in Las Vegas, the plane will be surrounded by government agents who will rush the plane and capture the messenger. When it becomes clear that the messenger was not acting alone, but that his flatulence was inspired by an enforced diet of beans and cabbage fed him by Albert and yourself, both of you will be seriously implicated. A vet, sympathetic to the canine cause, will act on Pablo's behalf, but Albert will be judged incompetent and sent directly home to me. Why don't you send him home now and avoid trouble later?"

While listening to Mother, I took a scarf from the drawer of my bureau, fastened it around my neck, put on my red velvet jacket and buttoned it, pushed my overnight case toward the door, and straightened my skirt.

"I want to talk to Pablo," Mother demanded. She would have liked to be the one who taught him to talk, but that was my accomplishment.

Pablo spoke into the receiver without growling.

| 91

His voice was high and clear, his throat a velvety passageway for sound since I had given him two lozenges made specifically for public speakers and singers (it was compounded from an original formula used by Enrico Caruso). "I love your daughter," Pablo said.

"Everybody loves her," Mother replied, "but nobody really knows her. She's a selfish monster, ungrateful, incapable of standing on her own two feet, keeps irregular hours, lives in a world of her own, lies, has a weak bladder, weak ankles, big ears, enormous feet, plaid shoulder caps, and her skin is host to a spy network of hidden capillaries. Now, do you still love her?"

Pablo spoke to her as one speaks to an angry child: obscurely. "Yes, dear Reverend, because I regard myself not as a victim engaged in some risky transcendental project, but rather as a lover who has absolutely no control over the forces that produce and distribute love. I am aware of Helen's qualities more than her faults: the rich variety of exciting games she makes up; the neatness of the papers upon which I perform my daily dislodging of waste; the endearingly simple way she opens a door halfway before coming in. Let me say this, I think it's normal for you as a mother to worry about Helen, but on the other hand you may be responsible for her failure which is as cumulative as lead poisoning, and forces her to rely on fantasy. Helen sees you as a madwoman commensurate with the pain you inflict. However I am here to see that it does not reach an unbearable intensity. It doesn't take a dog to understand the effect of conglomerate mergers such as father, mother, cousins, aunts, etcetera, versus the private enterprise of a child! In other words, Reverend Jones, Helen is trying to create her own life handmade. That should be sufficient profit for you as a mother."

"I will now speak to Albert," Mother declared.

Albert, trembling with fear, took the phone. He needed Mother's goodwill, was sure the plane would crash if she put her mind to wishing it would.

"Myra? Listen Myra, I'm not serious about Helen. Yes, I love you. Only you. This is just a short holiday I'm taking. Yes, I'll be lonely. Where are the pencils? Oh . . . I left them in a jar on the kitchen window. The paper is already cut into small pieces. Yes, there's a paperweight on the pile to keep it from flying in all directions when the door opens. You have three appointments tomorrow, check them out in your appointment book, the big one. What? No, of course Helen and I aren't eloping. I expect to win a great sum of money at the gaming tables. Don't cry. I am grateful to you. I'll bring you a souvenir from Las Vegas."

When Albert turned to me he was ashen. I brought him a glass of water. He was still hanging on to the phone, listening to Mother.

"She says I'm your half brother," he said in

horror. "What if we had slept with each other . . . or married and had children!"

I hit him. He needed it. "I'm ready to go now," he said.

"Albert, promise me you'll be a good sport in Vegas, and that you'll tell me if you start worrying about Mother, okay?"

"I promise."

55

On the plane, Albert tucked a blanket around me. He made sure I had a nap before dinner and sent back the cold chicken because it did not look fresh. I had instead a portion of pot roast drowning in gravy, with a side of instant mashed potatoes. The salad came with French dressing, artificially preserved and served in a tiny pleated plastic container. The flatware was sealed in a cellophane wrapper. Pablo had the best of it with a pound of raw sirloin steak brought from home. He consumed his food facing the window so that the stewardess would not notice the unusual slurping style he had of eating.

Albert explained our check-in procedure. "I have taken two single rooms, not adjoining, under two different names. You are the Countess Helena

De Jones, I am Meyer Wolfsheim the Third, and Pablo is Pablo De Jones Junior, your younger brother. The management will provide a cot for him in your bedroom. I've invited you, so the expenses are on me, the incidentals you are to take care of. I only tell you this to avoid unpleasant misunderstandings later."

56 The scene was bizarre. The Collonade Hotel was holding a Mexican fiesta party when we arrived. All the people I had ever read about in the society columns were there, or was I dreaming? I believe I saw Slap Threnody Lawless (dazzling in gold lamé), Eyesore & Chaste Revered (who wouldn't revere him?), Candy Rawhole (that's what happens when you have a sweet tooth), Silly Blah (it rhymes with *ah*), Gonad & Iodine Von Iceyburg (thawing out of course), Armwet & Cement Squirtgun (who recently bought an apartment overlooking the Champs de Bon Marché to put up all those wonderful rock stars who will just be passing through), Mrs. Puce Nimble (Puce be nimble, Puce be quick, Puce jump over the candlestick), Lacey Mirrorbell (bella, bella), Merry Schmutz (merrily, merrily, merrily, merrily, life is but a schmutzy dream), Mr. & Mrs. Robbers Skulk (what more can I say?), Saddy Sockaguy (the other side of the coin: remember Happy Rockefeller? of course you do), Mrs. Angier Fiddle-Puke (no, my dears, the disease is called angina), and the Baroness de Bologna-Salami, who sat around complaining that the telephone operators failed to deliver her messages, that the laundry did an inferior job and had starched her silk panties, but had put softener into her cuffs, and worst of all she said that the maid had a habit of bursting into her room at crack of dawn to see if she could make up the bed. The list is partial, of course, since I did not examine the hotel register.

After sending our bags up with a bellgirl (a small woman shaped like a bell, who had strong arms and wore a pillbox hat under which she carried all kinds of pills to sell to the Collonade's patrons), we went to the main ballroom. The director of entertainment was wearing a blue football helmet and carried a baseball bat; with this bat he advanced on a piñata shaped like a pig that was hanging from the ceiling. He then slammed the piñata till it split open and ten thousand dollars' worth of small gifts tumbled out of its belly. With a great shout and screams of delight, forty-two women, all expensively dressed and coifed, rushed toward the loot and began scrambling in the shredded paper that had been the papier-mâché beast's innards. It was a ridiculous riot, instigated by greed not need, everybody wanted something for nothing; they were actually being taken for a management promotional ride, and would be losing far more than they were getting, at the gaming tables later on. One woman, who was tickled by a man to make her let go of a package, slammed him in the face with it before stalking off. The man bled, but did not leave the field. Others came limping toward the velvet chairs that surrounded the ballroom. Hardly anyone remained uninjured.

Pablo peed in his pants with excitement. We moved to another spot. A dry one. Watched a Charleston contest. The most powerful woman in Las Vegas (politically powerful), who was the madam of a whorehouse, won a baroque silver serving tray for her abandoned performance, and a princess who had almost been thrown by her mount during the hobbyhorse competition received an emerald bracelet. I watched enviously as others carried off a white mink coat, a custom-designed men's watch from Tiffany's, and the key to an antique convertible Daimler. Lady Luck once smiled at me, too, when I sang the Campbell's soup jingle over the phone and received a case of tomato soup.

57 There were two croupiers at our single-ended table. As the roulette wheel turned, it made a sound like false teeth clicking. Albert put his chips on manque, betting that the winner would be between numbers one and eighteen. The croupier spun the wheel in a counterclockwise direction, then removing his hands, showed us that they were empty. When the wheel stopped he removed the ball from the winning compartment, keeping his hand turned so that we could see the ball at all times. Then he paid out. Albert did not win. *"Faites vos jeux,"* the croupier called, and while the ball was in motion we placed our bets again. This time Albert had put his chips on rouge. He lost anyway.

"Why don't we play the slot machines?" I asked. "You'll lose every cent if this keeps up." Albert agreed. He had brought only a few hundred dollars with him.

"I would have won," he complained, "if I had used the Sean Connery method."

"What's that?"

"Well, Connery won thirty thousand at Italy's Saint Vincent Casino by backing number seventeen three times."

"My grandfather had a more eccentric system," I said, remembering a family anecdote of how the Joneses recouped the family fortune after losing everything. "His equipment was a spider trapped in a matchbox that was painted half red and half black on the inside. He'd put the box in front of him on the table, remove the lid after a few minutes, and then bet on rouge or noir according to the spider's position."

"Where can I get a spider in Las Vegas?" Pablo asked.

"We might look in the cellar," Albert suggested.

58 Down in the subbasement we did find a spider's web, but the spider wasn't at home.

"Why don't we use a spider substitute?" I suggested.

"Like what?" Pablo asked. "A mouse?"

"You're close. . . . How about a cockroach?"

"Yes, that's it. We'll search for a roach. But what about the matchbox?" Albert said.

"Steal one from the kitchen," I answered.

"And the red and black paint, where do we get that?" Albert said.

"Use lipstick and eyebrow pencil." I showed them the huge selection of junk that I always carried with me in a zippered makeup case.

We fanned out. I found the roach. It was pregnant and sluggish, but nothing to get sentimental about. A pregnant roach brings good luck if you treat it kindly and say a prayer over its useless wings, which I did:

> cockroach, cockroach
> be a honey
> cockroach, cockroach
> bring us money
> Amen.

Albert stole the box of matches from one of the hotel's huge stainless steel kitchens. "These are a great temptation," he confided.

"Never mind, empty the matches into that mop sink, and let the water run over them," I said.

Albert was so docile I should have suspected something; instead I gave my attention to preparing the box.

Our high hopes, our preparations came to nothing. We lost. The second time around, before we had placed our bets, the cockroach crawled out of the box and climbed on a woman's hand. She screamed, and we were asked to leave the table. Albert seemed unusually agitated. He excused himself and went to the men's room.

"Follow him, Pablo!" I ordered.

Pablo could not find Albert in the men's room. We searched the lobby, the bar, and our bedroom, but no Albert.

"Let's try the subbasement, he might be returning the roach to its nest," I said.

That's where we found him, pouring Mazola oil over piles of dirty laundry. Pablo had to keep him at bay, while I went through his pockets for matches.

"You're arousing me," Albert warned. "Keep that up and I'll do something we'll both be sorry for."

"What's that, Albert?"

"I'll start a fire in your heart," he answered.

59

That night room service brought us a quart of rum raisin ice cream and three goblets of madeira. With his credit card Albert bought me a feather boa in the boutique. It was flame red.

"Remember, I'm your half sister," I cautioned. "Don't get carried away."

"I have a confession to make to you, Helen. Even if you weren't related to me I could never make love to you. I don't know what love is. I know what ice cream is. I know what a car it. But what is love?"

"Please, Albert, let's not discuss it. I was only foolin' around. Finish your ice cream."

By the time Albert had finished his madeira he was obnoxious. "Know why I don't like you, Helen?" he began.

"Why, Albert?"

"Because you oil your face at night, sleep in a torn nightgown, leave your bed unmade day after day, keep rotting apple cores in your ashtrays, walk barefoot, and sleep around.

Poor Albert, he was hallucinating. I hadn't "slept around" for a year . . . and what an expression. However, now I knew why Mother was his dish of tea, it wasn't because she was keeping him from the police and the psychiatric ward, it was because of her meticulously clean sheets, frilly nightgowns from Lord and Taylor's, and her clean feet.

60 "What did you learn in Las Vegas?" Daddy asked.

"I learned that *weight* is a measure related to heaviness by carrying away a pocketful of silver dollars. I learned that *length* is a measure of extent or distance by counting my footsteps from the lobby of the hotel to my bedroom. I learned that *volume* is a measure of space occupied when I filled my water glass to rinse my mouth. I learned that *temperature* is a measure of hotness or coldness when I felt my forehead and found that I had fever."

"I hope you didn't take an aspirin!" Daddy said.

"No, I didn't, Edward. The fever went away by itself the minute I got back to New York."

"And did you take my advice?" he asked.

"What advice, Edward?"

"The safety strategy," he said. "You remember . . . I told you how to protect yourself."

"Of course. It slipped my mind for a minute."

Daddy had warned me to leave my valuables in the hotel safe, and to bolt my door before retiring. Since Pablo was my only valuable I couldn't very well leave him in the hotel safe, but I had locked our door from the inside before going to sleep. Other things I did not do: I did not drink too much and so did not end up unconscious in the street minus my wallet. I did not take a taxi and give the driver directions only to find myself going in the opposite direction, and after surrendering my money dropped off far from my hotel. I did not let ragged children approach me, children whose charm is their chief tool, crying, "You are a nice lady, I like nice ladies. Please buy this flower." I couldn't imagine why Edward had chosen to worry about these particular things, unless he had consulted one of his out-of-date travelers' manuals. It is the proper thing for a father to warn his daughter of the perils that lie ahead. Edward does love me and wants me to be happy.

61 The following scene took place at Marian's apartment. I had brought an Italian bread and a container of ricotta for her, as a post-Vegas gift. When I rang the bell, Marian appeared.

"Hi, Marian," I said. "Look at what I brought you."

"I am not Marian," she answered, and slammed the door. I stood there for a moment not knowing what to do, and then decided to leave. Halfway down the stairs, I stopped and thought, "Wait a minute!"

Up the stairs I went and once more rang Marian's bell. Enraged by this continual ringing, Marian opened the door . . . but before she could say a word, I said, "I am not Helen either." And went downstairs again.

In a few days whatever it is will blow over.

62 I picked up the phone at the second ring. Sometimes I wait for the third; I do not want to seem too eager.

"Helen?"

"Speaking."

"The fear of death is a symptom of betrayal!"

"Who is this?"

"Nobody."

There was a click, a broken connection, and then dead air caught between myself and whom?

63

"Why are you doing this to me?" I asked Pablo. He had defecated on the floor and placed a tiny paper flag at the top of the pile.

"Don't take it personally. I was trying to re-create Iwo Jima from this photograph."

"But I have to clean up after you!"

"Enemy of self-expression!"

"Come clean Pablo, what's it really about?"

"My memories are intolerable, Helen. I guess I was seeking revenge for my sister who was treated poorly by your kind when she was just a pup."

"What do I have to do with it?"

"You're not an animal; you're a natural enemy."

"Nonsense. Haven't I always been kind to you?"

"Read this newspaper story. It might help you to understand my basic mistrust of forked creatures."

The clipping, yellowed and uneven, told a shocking story:

PUPPY BEATEN TO DEATH: OWNERS JAILED

A young Brooklyn couple was charged with murder last night in the fatal beating of their two-month-old dog. Police said Princess was beaten to death by her master, Richard Person, and her mistress, Nona, both 20.

The pup's body, covered from head to toe with cuts, welts, and bruises, was found yesterday in the backyard of the couple's apartment at 336 Heather St.

"She was hairless and black-and-blue from her forehead to her feet," said Detective Peter Rogers of the Alley Ave. station.

According to police, neighbors said the dog had been beaten almost every day for two weeks, but the beatings intensified over the weekend during an outdoor party and barbecue, when the dog stole a hamburger from the grill.

Detectives said Person hit the tiny animal with his fists and a belt, while the mistress also "used physical force."

On Sunday, the cops reported, the dog was forced to sit still in the rain, held by a metal choke collar attached to a fence.

Around 8:30 A.M. yesterday, Person drove his wife to a subway station, so she could go to her job as a computer trainee. Then he returned home and slept until noon.

When he awoke, police said, he found the puppy lying on the ground. Unable to rouse her, he called the A.S.P.C.A. and reported that the pup "doesn't wake up."

Person was advised to bring the pup in. When veterinarians Alfred Jonas and Ricardo Maldonado saw the body, they called for detectives to take over the investigation.

Police said the pup's legs were swollen, her face was puffed up, and her lips were three times the normal size.

The cops quoted Person as saying: "Princess wasn't housebroken. I was disgusted with her. . . . I wanted obedience from that dog and I didn't get it."

Detectives said that while Person was being questioned in the police station he shouted: "I want a lawyer. Get on the phone. I want my rights."

Person and his wife were booked on charges of murder, possessing a dangerous weapon (the belt), and endangering a pup's welfare.

64

"Must I be punished for what others of my species have done?" I asked Pablo.

"Yes you must, until I can feed the hand I bite."

Why couldn't Pablo get it into his head that I would always be his kind philanthropist and he would remain the needy petitioner? I reprimanded him for his own good.

"Bad dog! Bad dog! From now on scratch the

door when you have to go out, or you won't get any supper!"

65

65 I happened to be standing near the door when the note was slipped under it. The paper was a cloudy blue, watermarked, and 60 percent rag content.

> Dearest Watched Lady,
>   I know that you are ALONE! And if like me would need some cumponionship for 1 evng or few hour, I am willing to say nice thing! You are MODERN miss, so I been keep away till now! BUT IS READY! Hear this cumplete sentence, "HOW ARE YOU? I AM FINE." Tonite at 8 I have for you the best SURPRISE! Make you happy and smile to me!
>   Not be afraid of lonly old man.
>   Check my name at desk in lobby.
>   I have room here too.
>   Yrs Truly,
>   ROBERT DELFORD SMITH
>   alias
>   BOB FJORD SMYTHE
>   (which you prefer is available)

"Room 21B," the desk clerk said, "is occupied by one of our oldest tenants, Mr. Robert D. Smith, a senior citizen. He's harmless, toothless, and practically penniless. Some of our other guests have complained about him. Do you have a complaint?"

"No," I answered.

66

Curious, but apprehensive, I knocked at his door. I was not prepared for his terrifying and incongruous appearance: his hair was dark and greasy, curtaining his long, thin face. He wore horn-rimmed bifocals that were held together with adhesive tape and rubber bands. There were ragged gaps between his broken teeth through which he breathed heavily. His outfit, something out of grand opera, was made of thick navy flannel with rows of brass buttons down the front. It was much too big for him, so he had rolled up the sleeves at the cuffs, and the trousers around his ankles. On his bare feet were laceless shoes splitting open at the welts and seams. His hands were red and rough, with fingernails like talons, half an inch long and encrusted with dirt.

"Please to come in," he bowed deeply. "This is good room, no leaks, very romantic."

"I don't have much time," I said.

"Time is relevant," he replied.

"But I will come in for a few minutes."

"You will not be displaced. I promise."

In the dim light I made out another figure on an unmade cot. I was taken by the hand and led to it.

"Helen Jones, please meet my silent partner, your twin sister. Am I right?"

The figure on the cot was a large rag doll, made to look exactly like myself, and wore most of the clothing that I had found missing during the previous month: my Allura red wig with open-weave backing, my sweater, and my gold pants and jacket by Funky. She/it even had on my chunky green wedgies, her fat cloth ankles were swollen and looked as if they had the gout.

"How did you get my things?" I asked the old man, but not too harshly. I wanted to catch him off guard.

"I buy at great bargain from dog. He like butcher bone with some meat, and I like to make pretty companion. It was fair deal."

"What do you do with this . . . this dummy?" I asked. "Do you talk to it?"

"Talk. Hold. Go for walk around room like real person. When I want her to be warm, I put this in."

He pulled a hot water bottle out from under the doll's pants.

"Sometime I kiss her on lips, but am too old to be excite."

"I think you have great talent," I said, edging toward the door. "You might make yourself a whole family someday out of scraps."

Suddenly animated and spilling over with memories he shouted: "Talented? Yes! When little boy I was drawing apple and pear in school. They give paper, pencil, eraser. LOOK!" He grabbed a blackened pot off a hot plate. "Peas, carrots, potato, meat. They have no color. When I cook the color go away. It make me so sad."

"I'm sorry," I said. "Raw food *is* much prettier."

"But is all right," he said. "I make picture of food."

The old man pulled me back into the room, sat me on the bed, and made me look at thirty crayoned still lifes that he had drawn on the sides of brown bags and cardboard boxes. He was, without doubt, a late bloomer, a marvelous primitive.

"Now we celebrate," he said. "We eat."

It was hard for me to believe that this was the man who had written those dirty notes and called me on the telephone. However, when I thought about it, I came to the conclusion that Pablo had put him up to it, to get even with me. Robert Delford Smith had been a convenient scapegoat.

67 When I knocked on Mr. Smith's door the next day, there was no answer.

"They came and took him away," the desk clerk said.

"Who took him away?"

"Don't know. Could be some government agency arranged for him to go to an old people's home or a hospital. Wherever it is, he'll be better off."

68 Daddy's been showing movies at his house. The young people who come to him love movies. They gaze at the screen as if it were the Buddha's eyes behind which all things past and present occur. Sometimes Daddy shows Chaplin shorts, and old comedies like *Behind the Eightball*. Once an eight-minute film taught how to make a bomb out of a bottle instead of a lamp out of a bottle. Lamps, the narrator said, were only good to hit husbands on the head with while they were sleeping, but Molotov cocktails (the bottle-bombs) could wipe out a blockful of enemies. Mostly the films are chosen because of their cheap rental. This sometimes leads to unfortunate juxtapositions: Betty Boop cartoons followed by male stag movies, followed by a lesson on how to bake a Key Lime pie.

When I visited Edward he was presenting the world premiere of a film concerning psychosurgery: *Before and After Psychosurgery.*

"The psychosurgeons are up to some pretty horrifying things nowadays," Daddy said. "I am haunted by one aspect of this technique, the participation of the 'psychotherapist,' who literally sits beside his patient conducting an interview with him while the neurosurgeons gradually turn up the electrical current. In this manner the 'therapist' monitors and titrates the amount of tissue destruction required to change the patient's ongoing emotional reactions. The patient himself cannot tell what's happening, since destruction of the frontal lobe tissue is reflected in a progressive loss of all those human functions related to the frontal lobes: insight, empathy, sensitivity, self-awareness, judgment, emotional responsiveness, and so on."

The movie in black and white was shown using the split-screen technique. On one side, a black woman wearing a self-stimulation unit on her belt turned it on and off as she wandered about a hospital. She was pressing the buttons in a frantic fashion because it built her up toward a feeling of orgasm that she was not able to consummate. This particular woman's problem, a narrator reported, was narcolepsy, a tendency to fall asleep unexpectedly in inappropriate situations, e.g., when seated on the toilet, standing on a crowded train platform, or slicing a roast with a sharp kitchen knife. . . . Since she wore her self-stimulation unit on her belt, her friends or other patients could simply press her wake-up button for her when she began to doze off. The other side of the screen showed a woman being stimulated electrically: she reported a pleasant tingling sensation in the left side of her body "from my face down to the bottom of my legs." She started giggling and making funny comments, stating that she enjoyed the sensation very much. . . . Finally, becoming more flirtatious, she ended up by openly expressing her desire to have sexual intercourse with the therapist.

Next, an eleven-year-old boy, otherwise normal, became so terribly excited by the electrical stimulation that he decided he would like to be a girl . . . and . . . on the other side of the split screen, much to my horror, I saw Mr. Smith, my neighbor, with electrodes springing out of his head like a sparkling Las Vegas headdress. The investigator made him dance, masturbate, and grin at the camera like a monkey. Finally, because his pleasure and pain centers had been irritated by the remote control device, he wept and fell down, totally exhausted.

A therapist, his hands hidden in the pockets of his crisp white smock, reported: "Although Mr. Smith is somewhat senile and nonproductive, he has undergone a very dramatic change. He is now co-operative and easily managed, but still not productive." As the camera moved in for a close-up of Mr. Smith's face, he spoke: "I guess, doctor, that your electricity is stronger than my will."

69 I'm going crazy. Pablo is gone. He left no note. I'm inclined to believe he's on his way to Hollywood to become a star. He doesn't have it in him to become a watchdog; too easily distracted. It runs in his family. His grandfather, he told me, disappeared for one entire evening after hearing that Halley's comet was coming and with it the end of the world. The old dog, then a young pup, had climbed onto the roof of a building because he wanted to see the end of the world happen. From the roof where he was waiting, he had an unobstructed view of the sky. He told Pablo that before the comet appeared words had materialized in the sky saying: IT IS I. His grandfather was amazed by the perfect use of grammar, it convinced him that God was an educated doG whose command of English could save the world . . . and that if all doGs practiced correct usage of the language the dog pounds of the world would soon be emptied. Needless to say, the world did not end with Halley's comet, and Pablo's grandfather was beaten by his master. Could Pablo have gone to the roof in search of another comet? Another message? Another fulfillment of the recurrent prophecy that the world is about to end?

70 Pablo was not on the roof.

71 I called on Mother to learn his fate. She began her psychic search by asking for and receiving an object belonging to Pablo, his old tennis ball (his favorite possession).

"I am getting vibrations of the route they took," she said.

"He's with someone?"

"Don't interrupt. Yes, he is with a dark-complexioned man from the East. The man is coming out of a notions shop with a skein of red wool and a box of straight pins. They go to a hotel. It has a a neon sign. I may be wrong. It may not be a hotel. Something else. Perhaps a store. It's not close. Quick, give me a map of New York City!"

I gave Mamma the map of N.Y.C. that I carried with me in order to pretend I was a tourist. I can't count the times I've searched for Grand Central Station and found it, first on my map, and then on Forty-second Street. It's always a surprise, like discovering an Egyptian tomb in the Metropolitan Museum of Art.

Mamma traced a route south toward Houston Street, the area called SoHo, where there are many galleries, artists, and restaurants.

"Yes, the sign is in the window of a store. . . . Some kind of gathering is taking place. I can feel it. He is here. *Here!*" Her finger stopped close to Prince Street.

72

I put up signs everywhere describing Pablo and giving my phone number. So far nobody has contacted me.

73

The surprise guest at our local supermarket was announced on a big piece of paper glued to the window: *Joe Fafka!* He was pushing a product called Daley's Instant Cheese. (Daley's comes in powder form and is good to take on camping trips or wherever an instant cheese is needed. All that has to be done to the powder is to add some water to the mixture and squeeze in the plastic pouch included in the package. This forms a doughlike ball which tastes like a nutty Swiss.) At last I would meet Joe in person. I was already waiting in front of the cardboard display when Joe came in the door. He was wearing a green silk suit, had a round childlike face, and stood about five feet two inches. He stood up on the box provided for him behind the display and spoke into the microphone: "To any lady who tries our product today, while I am here, a free ticket to visit our radio studios and take the grand tour! See your favorite radio personalities who have *never* been seen before. Watch them in action: see them walk, talk, check the clock, drink coffee from a paper cup. All this and more if you'll step up and make your purchase. Also included in each and every package of Daley's Instant Cheese is a coupon allowing you a five-cent discount on your next package. Folks, this cheese doesn't taste like instant anything, it tastes like an authentically aged cheese. It's a quality cheese. Daley's can also be stored without refrigeration. Put it in the kiddies' lunch bag and let them develop their grip while they squeeze the cheese. And yes, we stand behind our product, there's a money-back guarantee for those of you who do not agree with us that Daley's is the cheese of the future, the cheese the moon should have been made of, the cheese that is the *best* money can buy. Now really folks, you have everything to gain and nothing to lose. Step right up. Our pretty cheese saleswoman is standing by to offer you a sample of Daley's right now."

A woman wearing a bunny costume minus the ears and tail began smearing cheese on tiny squares of crackers.

"Who is he?" a woman asked. "Is he famous or somethin'?" Her cart was full of beer, crackers, bologna, and cheese. Joe spotted her in the crowd, pointed to her, and said, "You, madame, must be giving a party, am I right?"

"Yes I am," she replied.

"Then let me add to the total enjoyment of your party by presenting you with a generous sample of Daley's Instant Cheese." With that, he threw two packages of Daley's into her cart. A few women applauded. Joe took a bow.

I waited till Joe was done and had autographed all the scraps of paper that were thrust upon him. Then I followed him to the back of the store where the manager was gifting him with three porterhouse steaks.

"Joe, I've gotta talk to you. I have a serious problem. . . . I called you last week."

"Not here, stupid," he hissed.

"It can't wait," I pleaded. There were tears in my eyes. The manager tried to shove me but I wouldn't move.

"This is private back here, girlie," the manager said. "Employees only."

Something about me must have attracted Joe, because once he had the bag of meat under his arm, his mood changed. "I have time for a coffee. You can spit it out over coffee, kid, but don't think I'm God. I'm not."

"I know you're not, Joe. I agree with you."

74

We went to a vegetarian restaurant on Seventy-ninth Street. I had tea with an apple strudel, and Joe had coffee with a cheese Danish. "I don't usually break bread with a nut," he said. "What's the story?"

"I've lost a loved one. . . ."

"Then it's too late for me to help." Joe bit into his Danish. "Not a bad piece of cake."

"Lost, not dead, Joe. And I've tried just about everything: put an ad in the paper, put posters around, walked my feet off. . . ."

"This loved one . . . is he your husband?"

"Not exactly."

"What do you want the jerk back for? He's not worth taking back. The same thing would start all over again, the beatings, the arguments over money, the drunken weekends. . . ."

"He's not a jerk and he never acted the way you say, Joe."

"He's not a drinker?"

"Absolutely not."

"What you're telling me is that he was a good man and you suspect foul play. Am I right?"

"Partly."

"Fill me in. Oh, and try to catch the waiter's eye, will you, honey? I could go for another pastry."

"He's not a man, my loved one isn't—"

"Not a woman! Jesus Christ, I hope you're not a dike. They live miserable lives. Don't tell me I'm having coffee with an invert."

Another pastry arrived. Joe sent it back. He had lost his appetite.

"Here's a picture of Pablo," I finally said. "We were very close. I know you're an animal lover and an antivivisectionist, so I came to you."

Joe's mouth hung open. "You got the wrong guy, honey. I'm a hunter. Ed Evans who comes on after me is the animal lover. I'm allergic to dogs and cats. I swell up and can't breathe when they get near me."

"You've got to help me. Your listeners can help. I want you to broadcast a description of Pablo— that's his name—and then maybe someone'll call in who's seen him."

To get me off his back, Joe agreed to appeal to his people.

75 Mother had been cleaning out her boxes and bags that contained old letters, bills, memorabilia of her fantastic psychic performances, phone numbers of friends long gone, Christmas cards, newspaper clippings, old keys, childhood photographs, compositions on yellow, lined paper, useless discount coupons, paper clips, and brittle rubber bands; in this conglomeration of junk she found a diary I had begun in the sixth grade, and sent it to me. Her reason for sending it was to hurt me. The first few lines read as follows: "I'm going into 7th grade. In a very tough Junior High School. It is Aug. 16, and I have not recieved my card from the new school telling me what class I'm to be in. I hope I've made an honor class. Somehow all this I'm writing sounds very boring & stupid. Well anyway to get on about the school. It is a very big school and has a lot of unfriendly children. I really enjoyed my old school P.S. 173. I hope I'm as popular in 115 as I was in 173."

I called Mother. "Why did you send me that diary?" I asked.

"It's yours, I didn't want to throw it out."

"You've thrown out other things of mine . . . the teddy bear, my first hair curler . . . things I loved. Why call my attention to the unhappy past?"

"Learn from it. Learn from the past. It should make you realize that you always were a worrier. Before you even set foot in the new school you had talked yourself into believing the children there would be unfriendly to you."

"Turned out they were."

"You're the unfriendly person, Helen. People react to you. If you were friendly, you'd be well liked. That's why you don't have friends even now."

"You're tearing me down again, Mother. Cut it out!"

"We've never talked woman-to-woman, dear. Why don't you drop over tonight? I apologize for being tactless."

"It isn't that you lack tact, Mother, but rather that you hate me and can't admit it to me, or to yourself. Now you want me to visit you so that you can continue your attack. I won't come."

"I want to see you, Helen," Mother said. Her voice sounded tired and sad. Could she be lonely for me? Had I been too harsh? Still I held back.

"It's too late," I said.

"Please, dear, your own mamma wants to hold her darling little Helen."

All right, Myra, I won't be long."

76 Mother was sitting in the dark, candles out, chairs still set up from the previous session. The room seemed gripped with bitter cold. . . . It may have been her mood. The steam was on. It knocked and hissed as it came out of the small pressure valve attached to the radiator. As Mother moved, her chair creaked. Soon she became visible as well as audible. In the dimness her form took on the insubstantial shape of a being not yet finished . . . a cold, gray lump that had materialized out of the vague light.

"I do not protect sinners, even though that sinner might be myself," she whispered. "I have summoned you here to confess a wrong."

"What're you up to now, Myra?" I asked. She had the unnerving habit of staging her communications so that the other person became uneasy. I found myself drifting into a hypnotic state . . . hypnotic or . . . dreamy with an edge of fear: what if I slipped away into the gossamer ambience and could not get back? "Mind if I put on the lights?" I flipped the switch before she could answer.

The cold, gray lump stood up, motionless.

"Son of a bitch!" she said. "You have no sense of theater. Don't you realize how hard it is to say certain things? I require the proper setting."

Mother glared at me. I stood my ground. The lights would remain on.

"I don't have long to live," she began again, trying for my sympathy. I had heard it before.

"Nobody has long to live, Mother. Life is short."

"And," she continued as if I had not interrupted her, "and, I have sent Albert away. He was too frivolous, more of a liability than I wanted to be responsible for."

"Where have you sent him?"

"Where? Away. He is being taken care of by those more conversant with his pleasures. It may be expensive, but where he is now Albert has his own asbestos-lined room with a clearly marked escape route that leads directly to either a homey recreation area or to his doctor's spacious recording studio."

"Myra, I didn't come here to talk about the expensive rest home you've sent Albert to. His therapy means nothing to me. I came because you sounded human and I miss my mommy."

She shifted from foot to foot. "Would you like a cup of tea with some strawberry jam and crackers?"

Tea with Myra was like playing house with a giant doll. I had owned a tea set when I was a child (the exact duplicate of Mother's). My teapot had a tea cozy, which is a flannel outer wrapping, to keep the water in the pot hot. The mention of a cup of tea made me vulnerable, took me back to when I had adored Myra and imitated her social graces.

"Yes, I'd love some tea," I replied, reaching out for Myra's hand to hold it affectionately. She let her hand lie in mine like a flattened kippered herring. All emotion had been scraped from the bones, and love smoked out. "I'm a commodity," the hand seemed to say, "a delicacy that will soon be gone. Have me while you can. The supply of mothers' hands is growing low."

Behind the door I heard her humming happily as she put the water up to boil and took out the dishes.

"I miss you," she said on returning. "Nobody can take the place of a daughter."

"I'm sorry, but you'll have to get along without me. I have my own life to live."

Her body heat bundled me closer to her in the cold room. I began to sweat. What would she say now to keep me from escaping?

"I remember you before you remember yourself," she said, her eyes reflecting the jubilation of the past. "I remember the drunken joy I felt at your birth. . . . I had an orgasm at the height of pain. . . . You wanted to remain, but I opened my womb and then in the cool white mist of the delivery room gave birth. First you were a flowerlike form bound to me only by the slenderest stem. The stem shriveled as the human flower ripened. You were my first miracle."

I mixed strawberry jam into my tea. The strawberries settled at the bottom of the cup. "Can you read strawberry fragments the way you read tea leaves?" I asked.

"The strawberry does not lend itself to interpretation," she answered wearily. I suppose she was disappointed in me. I should have praised her for accomplishing my birth, for feeling both pleasure and pain where only pain was to be expected. I kept my strategic distance.

"I have to go soon, Myra." My using her name instead of calling her Mother made her realize that I would not come any closer.

Then we sat silently. I wanted to leave. She was eager to have me stay with her in the eerie, "prepared" room.

"When you were eight years old you had a dog named Scamp. You were very attached to her. She ate your leftovers, slept in your room, went to school with you, in short was your best friend. One afternoon while you were away at school, Scamp disappeared. I told you that she had run away. She didn't!" Mother's face hardened, as she reintroduced an old trauma.

"What happened to Scamp?" I heard myself cry, in that anguished child's voice from the past.

"I took her for a walk and left her in the street. I hated her! She tore up the rugs, dirtied the house with those 'cute' muddy paws, made too much noise, and cost too much money. You and that dog gave me extra work; if I could have left *you* on the street with the dog and been guaranteed I'd never see you both again, I would have. At the age of eight you took over my life. Mine! You demanded everything:

time, love, money. Oh, I felt great when I got rid of Scamp. It was like springtime. I could live again!"

"And Edward?" I couldn't believe that Daddy had been part of the plot.

"Oh, your father wanted me to keep Scamp. It was easy for him to be the good guy; he wasn't ever at home to take care of Scamp. Your father is an old softy."

"You've always been so devious, Myra," I said quietly. "You should have been a surgeon; you operate with brilliance. Now tell me, what else have you taken away from me that I loved?"

"Nothing. I've taken nothing!" My pain gave her strength; it brought color to her face. "Didn't you want Edward to hate me? Aren't you still working on it?" I thought I was controlling myself very well, though if Myra hit me where it really hurt, somewhere in the vicinity of Pablo's disappearance, I would have struck her.

"Edward isn't the angel you think he is," Myra shouted. "I'm a better person than he'll ever be."

"I'm aware of his faults," I answered.

"Oh, are you? Well, how would you like to go to bed with a flaccid floral arrangement? That's what he was with me in bed—a dead bloom, a twisted wreath. . . ."

"That's your private business, Myra," I said. It broke my heart to hear it.

77   The unvoiced can be heard as clearly
as the voiced, but we do not have to pay attention
to it . . . until insanity overtakes us.

78   All living things, including human
babies, get destructive radiations from their mothers;
those radiations might underlie "hate at first sight."
People with "brown thumbs" emit radiations harm-
ful to their plants.

79   When I bought half a rye bread at the
bakery, the salesperson gave me the smaller half.
I was too embarrassed to ask to see the other half
close up, to measure it against my half. I did not
want to seem greedy. But it was my money I spent.
I should have asserted myself. Since Pablo has gone,
I almost welcome unfair treatment. Unhappiness and
a sense of loss have to be fed or they lessen in in-

| 129

tensity. I must be careful not to smile. To smile is to deny my daily mourning. I don't want to embark on another life (I don't dare to be happy) until I find Pablo.

80

Jeremy, Marian's old man, does not look like Mick Jagger (Marian says he does because of his thick lips and tall skinny frame). Maybe in a jump suit he'd come closer . . . but until then he's only Mick Jagger in Marian's head.

"Marian, you're lucky to have an old man and a young baby. I don't think I can make it without Pablo."

"I had my hard times," she said. "Things still aren't that good."

"What'dya mean?"

"Sex . . . I'm not really interested. Right after the baby I lost the urge. Remember how I used to ball all the time? Now nothing. It's not fair to Jeremy."

"No such thing as fair. How does that saying go? The body's willing but the mind says no?"

"Ain't no such saying, Helen. You know, Jeremy's a good man, but the sight of him doesn't make me jump for joy. We've become the little old couple at home. I don't get around the way I used to. I miss those pretty young boys who hang around Phoebe's. I don't need this . . . this security shit. It's shit. What can I write my songs about . . . diapers? Fifth-floor walk-up? My man's a road manager, hi-ho where does he go? My hands got red when I made the bed? I'm dying on the vine. I'm not even interested in clothes any more. Me! Dig this closet."

She opened the closet door. Hanging there good as new were tons of beautiful clothes; each dress had it own padded hanger, the sweaters were neatly folded on the shelf, and shoes were stacked in their original boxes.

"Never wear 'em. They just take up space," she said.

Jeremy, who had been mashing carrots for Elmer Joy, looked up and said: "Why don't you give your glad rags to Helen if they don't make you glad?"

"Right, take what you want," she offered. "Maybe with some freaky threads and a wig you'll feel differently about yourself."

I refused her offer because I couldn't see how clothes would make a new woman of me. Clothes hadn't helped Albert—he was back in the nut-burg again—and Pablo with his fancy gear had gone and left me all alone. Besides, Marian was not a generous person. If I accepted her wardrobe, she might renege and want the stuff back again. Then our relationship would consist of the transportation and maintenance of clothing. It might prove exhausting and time-consuming.

"I'm thinking of moving out of the Buckminster," I said.

"To where?"

"Not sure . . . East Side maybe . . . in the Seventies. I've never shared an apartment with another woman. . . . Could be a big help financially and socially."

"Yeah, you'll move when I get my first golden record," Marian said.

"Don't you believe me?"

"No."

She was right. It would take a bomb to get me out of the Buckminster. What if Pablo came trotting back some day?

"You staying for dinner?" Jeremy asked.

"I've got to get to sleep early, so I can wake up early. Joe Fafka is asking his listeners to watch out for Pablo. He's doing it as a public service."

"You know I don't believe in psychoanalysis, Helen," Marian said, "but in your case I think it would help. You're so hung up you're still wearing the hanger. Dig it, baby, what you need is a big, big change."

"And what you need is to write songs again. I think your life as it is right now is interesting enough material to write about. Why do you put it down?"

"Don't change the subject. We're talking about Helen Jones now, not Marian Freylinghusen Von Hoffer. I know I can write the shit out of any situation. I'm not worried about me. What does your mother say?"

"Mother!" Marian had never mentioned my mother before.

"Yeah, mother . . . I'm selfish, I don't want to be the only one suffering through this with you. Suffering's what mothers are for."

"Gee, Marian, I thought you hated my mother, too. Didn't we agree that she's an envious old fart who's jealous of me because I'm so thin?"

"Helen, Helen, Helen," Marian sighed. "Grow up."

Jeremy put his arm around my shoulder. "Don't let it get you down. There are worse things in the world. When I was a kid, my dad took me fishing. We were both crazy about angling, and we had a wonderful day catching trout and pickerel. Man, suddenly it got dark, and we decided to take a shortcut to where the car was. We had to cross a swamp, you know, full of fallen trees. Had to climb up one trunk to get to the other side of the swamp. Didn't notice the water moccasin curled up in front of us, a nasty creature. Then wherever we turned there were snakes curling and slithering. We couldn't go back and we couldn't go forward. We managed to hook the snakes directly in front of us on the log with our poles. The hooks broke with the weight of the snakes, but we jumped off the log just in time, as other snakes began to crawl on from the swamp, and were able to reach our car. I still get nightmares about it. That's bad stuff, see?"

"Thanks, Jeremy," I said, "but I don't get the connection."

"The connection is," Marian explained, "that Jeremy is on speed and can't stop talking."

"I'm coming down now," Jeremy said.

Marian put Elmer Joy into my arms as a gesture of friendship. "Kiss him," she said. "Kissing babies is as good as meditation."

Babies are so comforting. They smile all over their bodies and put their soft fingers into your mouth as if it is their own. They smell good, and laugh at funny faces.

I left in better shape than when I had arrived. Good friends are worth more than money, analysis, or a trip to romantic places.

81

Had no luck with the Joe Fafka program. His listeners thought he was putting them on about a talking dog. Who would want to be caught in broad daylight questioning a dog and waiting for an answer? There were some false leads: a Great Dane found in an abandoned car at One hundred thirty-eighth Street and Convent Avenue, a toy poodle caught between buildings on the Lower East Side, a nondescript dirty-white mutt who had been frightening children in the park at Ninety-Sixth Street near the horse path, and a Russian wolfhound that had run away from an outdoor photography session. Some sympathetic dog lovers offered pups from their dog's next litter. Joe invited me on the air to thank his many listeners. I began by expressing what I believed to be my warm and grateful feelings, but soon descended to the unpleasant sort of remarks one is apt to make when one has been abandoned. I fell apart.

"Joe, I want to thank your kind listeners for going all out for me and trying to find Pablo. Their words of comfort will always remind me that the milk of human kindness still flows, even though it soon becomes sour and stinks. How can so many of you folks listening in think that I am just like you? Even when I had Pablo, I didn't let him dirty the sidewalk. I don't prefer dogs to people. I never called him 'sweetsie pie,' or bought him matching rainboots, raincoat, and umbrella. I knew that Pablo was a dog. A dog is incapable of love. I was well aware that Pablo was with me for one reason, custodial care! I did not carry a photo of him in my wallet, nor is he my sole heir. My search for Pablo has nothing to do with the extremes of loneliness. If he does not return to me, there are other life-styles to investigate. His disappearance was a blessing in disguise. It freed me. I'll be able to take vacations without worrying about placing the dog. I'll be able to live wherever I want. My guests won't have to ask, 'Does he bite?' Pablo, if you are listening to this broadcast, I want you to know it's all over between us. You had the best of both worlds, yet you left without even a word of thanks. But I say to you—THANK YOU PABLO! THANK YOU FOR THROWING ME INTO THE POOL TO TEACH ME HOW TO SWIM!"

Callers flooded the lines insulting me. One woman said that if she ever met me she'd shave the hair off my head and make me walk nude down Broadway with a sign around my neck reading TRAITOR. There was one obscene call in which the man described himself as well hung, young, and dying of bitches. He was cut off before he reached a wider audience than myself.

Joe complimented me: "You contributed to a lively show. Thanks, Miss Jones. Interest is gonna run high for a long time."

"I enjoyed being on the show. I'd like a dialogue show myself. Is it hard?"

"Miss Jones, all you need is the gift of gab, a research assistant, and a strong viewpoint. Anyone can be a Joe Fafka, or a Pia Lindstrom, or even the McCanns at Home. . . . The bigger the job, the easier it is."

"How would I apply for such a job? I mean, where do I begin?"

"Can you write?" Joe asked. "You must be able to make sense on paper."
"I can write up a storm," I said.

82

I tried to write up a storm, just to see if I could. You don't get famous overnight, you've got to work at it.

Disaster Area

Storm Maxine blew up over the East Coast yesterday, destroying all that was in her path. For miles around, rubble was strewn over an area that once contained a prosperous business and residential community. Hundreds of lives were lost, along with millions of dollars' worth of property. Maxine, erratic and volatile, followed in her sister's path (last year Lorraine caused the President to declare the East Coast a national disaster area, and allocated thousands of dollars to rebuilding the seacoast). Weather forecasters say that Maxine and Lorraine are mysteries to them, since they did not follow the usual storm patterns, but erupted unexpectedly and with unforeseen fury, only to disappear in a few hours after the damage was done. "Just like a woman," was the comment heard, though strictly off the record, by those interviewing the President. He seemed in good spirits after a night of needed rest, and promised to support research designed to tame those "terrible ladies of death and destruction."

83 They called it superrealism, but it was Pablo. I had wandered down to SoHo, to the place on the map that Myra had pointed out, and there he was in a gallery, next to the store with a neon flying cock in the window.

An artist had made life-size exact replicas of my dog sleeping, humping a bitch, springing to the attack, eating, sniffing a tree, carrying a newspaper, sitting behind the wheel of a car (that was something new!). On the wall beside each piece of art was a page of information concerning Pablo. I was not mentioned.

The name of the artist was Luis Farash. I had seen his work before on the cover of *Time* magazine. His number was in the phone book and I called him immediately.

"Your dog?" the voice said. "Can you prove it?"

"I have pictures of him."

"Many dogs look alike. Are there any distinguishing features that would set him apart?"

"He answers to the name Pablo, and he can talk."

"Talk? All by himself without external manipulation of the voice box?"

"Sings too, though his repertoire is limited."

"Does he limp slightly and have one chewed ear?"

"Yes, an adolescent injury."

"I can see you know the dog well, Miss. . . ."

"Helen Jones."

"Miss Jones. The dog I have fits your description."

"Where do you live? I'll come right over to get him."

"I wouldn't do that if I were you."

"Why not?"

"He's happy here. . . . He's mine now. . . . The best model I've ever had."

"Let me speak to him."

"All right, but don't say I didn't warn you."

After a short pause, during which I heard whispering and giggling at the other end of the line, Pablo's voice reached me: "Helen? How ya doin' babe? I meant to drop you a note explaining. . . ."

"Explaining what?"

"That every dog must have his day . . . know what I mean?"

I didn't know what he meant. "Come off it Pablo, you drove me crazy wondering whether you were dead or alive."

"So now you know. I'm alive and happy. Happier than I've ever been. Luis has made me famous; we have a movie contract, a dog food endorsement, something in the works for a TV series, and next month T-shirts with my name and photograph will be on sale at May's department store exclusively."

Luis Farash took the phone and spitefully added, "I'm surprised you never helped Pablo realize his talents."

"Exploit him you mean."

"How did you find me?" This time a note of admiration in Pablo's voice.

"Myra helped; she told me where to search. I popped into the gallery, and there you were."

"How did you like the show?" Pablo asked as if I were just anyone who had happened to visit the gallery.

"Fuck you!" I shouted, and slammed the receiver down.

84 She who lies down with dogs gets fleas.

85 Farash's show, when I was able to be honest with myself, was upsetting and extremely moving because of his masterful skill. He had presented Pablo without a veneer of glamour, with complete verisimilitude. One might look upon his exhibition as an allegory of the basic needs of man unhampered by his superego. Watching a dog do what men do behind closed doors is a sight that engages one's sympathy and anger. Pablo was not heroic for he was only exhibiting his nature. But Luis Farash deserved four stars for daring such an overwhelming criticism of man's best friend. I wrote a letter to the Op-Ed page of the *Times,* enlarging on the above topic and recommending the show to incipient art lovers and other minorities. For this expansive attitude on my part I received an unexpected award. The letter of notification arrived in the mail this morning.

It is my honor to name you, on behalf of Altruistic Foundation, a recipient of the

| 141

Foundation's Altruist-in-Residence Award for 1974. This award is made in recognition of your sustained contribution to American moral growth through altruism; and it is intended as further encouragement to you, the generous citizen, to continue to give—with the tools of imagination, wit, pathos, and poetry—the personal and societal questions of human value and morality which illuminate a vigorous altruism and mirror the aspirations and searchings of a people striving for self-abnegation.

John H. Johns

86 Love takes a long time to wear off. I haunted the places where Pablo might be: Houston Street, Spring, West Broadway. In my shoulder bag I carried a jeweled collar for him. He was a sucker for hip jewelry, and might be won over. When I finally ran into him a few weeks later I didn't recognize him. Pablo had gained so much weight that he waddled. His eyes were blood shot and he could barely drag himself to the Spring Street bar.

"Aren't you taking care of yourself?" I asked.

"Farash buys me Nesselrode pie, ice cream, Sacher tortes, and whipped potatoes. I can't resist," he whispered hoarsely.

"You'll eat yourself to death!"

"I'm a social eater, not a foodaholic," he declared. "When I start hiding chocolate cake in the clothes hamper, then I'll go for help."

Luis Farash protested that he needed a fat Pablo since "Obesity and What Comes After" was the theme of his next show.

"You're a cruel man," I cried.

"No . . . I'm an artist," he said.

87 Through the window of the bar I could see Pablo being adored by two young women who were eating chicken crepes in cream sauce. They fed him choice bits of the succulent meat as he lay under their feet. Luis Farash took the check.

88 A Buckminster acquaintance, James McCrory, brought a bottle of wine and we drank it while watching a drama written especially for television. I had the blues and the creeps and needed company. The plot of the program went like this: a rabid dog is trapped in a heatless farmhouse. With him in the house is a family—a young boy, mother, father, and grandmother. There is a blizzard outside (natch). The father wants to shoot the dog. The little boy begs him not to do it. The dog bites the boy and the father shoots the dog. The grandmother has a heart attack, and the mother goes into labor pains. The snow blows under the door. The new infant is born. One by one the occupants of the house freeze to death. Finally only the father and the infant are alive. The father wraps the infant in everybody's clothing. He then shoots himself in the head. A helicopter lands and rescues the baby. Thirty-five years later we see the baby now grown into a man. He looks just like his father. He enters his home in an upper-middle-class suburb, finds his wife with a lover in flagrante delicto in the bedroom, takes a gun out of the bureau drawer, shoots her and her lover, then shoots himself in the head. We hear a baby cry, then see the little one in a crib in the bedroom. The end.

When the credits zoomed by I caught James McCrory's name as head writer. "You son of a gun!"

I exclaimed. "Why didn't you tell me it was your program?"

James kissed me and said, "I wanted to surprise you, get your gut reaction."

"I loved it, James. You're a great comic talent."

"Comic?"

"Comic, tragic, it's all the same. Haven't you ever heard the song 'I'm Laughin' with Tears in My Eyes'?"

"You hated it, didn't you?"

"No, no, I really loved it. It touched me, James, especially when the helicopter landed. I thought: 'Oh my God, he's too late!' What was it like to write it?"

"I had constipation, took dexies, worked around the clock, suffered headaches, lived like a monk in a trunk."

"If I wrote something, would you read it? You're the only professional author I know."

"I'm at your disposal m'lady, and will be happy to give you a criticism and evaluation for free . . . well, not exactly for free. . . . I want another kiss."

"That's easy," I said, all warm and cheerful.

"What are you going to write? Do you have a project in mind?"

"I kind of thought I'd write a story of unrequited love, sort of autobiographical . . . but it all comes out good in the end. Or do you think it should come out tragic?"

"That's up to you."

145

"Oh yeah. It is. Besides, if it's autobiographical it would have to be the truth . . . and I don't even know the end yet."

"No, you don't."

89 What is writing?

Imagine an ant colony carrying one by one a bit of food to their nest. The crumb of sustenance is bigger and heavier than any of the ants, yet they manage. They forage everywhere for their food; it is the instinct to survive. What others reject, they collect. Nothing is wasted.

This is not writing. It is comparison shopping.

90 Yes, I'd marry James. He's a darling mess. He likes me a lot. More than that. This time I'll play hard to get. I've learned that the best way to keep someone you love is not in a pumpkin shell

(pumpkin shells go soft and shrink). The thing to do is to keep one's emotions hidden, to be like Daddy's jade snail—valuable, art-carved, silent . . . coveted. I gave Pablo everything I had. Oh shit!

91 Marian and Jeremy have moved to Woodstock. Boy, did she luck into it. And now they'll live happily ever after.

92 Mother and I feel that Daddy has changed. He has proposed a grandiose scheme to the city art commission. It is the idea of an egomaniac: he wants to donate a 125-foot-high stainless steel Shirley poppy in full bloom showing its reproductive organs. If the idea is accepted, it will rise from a block-long bed of ordinary flowers on the center mall of Park Avenue between Sixty-eighth and Sixty-ninth Streets.

"It is totally inappropriate," Mother said, "and

a traffic hazard, besides. The sun shining off the stem and petals would blind drivers."

"Edward hates cars," I said. "It might be his diabolic plan to cause chaos and confusion. I'll try to talk him out of it."

93

"They have accused me of self-aggrandizement!" Daddy shouted. "They say what I want to do is similar to what the pharaohs used to do."

"They're right, Edward; you do have a pretty big monument in mind. Couldn't you just donate a bed of tulips, plant an empty lot somewhere? What's got into you?"

Daddy shrugged off my criticism. "I prefer to do the unusual. You know that, Helen. I've never gotten a kick out of giving five thousand dollars here and five thousand dollars there."

94   Word got out about Daddy's offer to
the city, and Joe Fafka's program was inundated by
calls from indignant citizens who wanted to air their
views.

"Joe, do you think it's right for a private citizen
to use a public avenue to put up a work of art so-
called?"

"No sir, I don't," Joe began, "and this particular
statue is another political move by those gay libera-
tion creeps who want to deflower the innocent. The
monument is at least eight feet wide and a hundred
and twenty-five feet high . . . a monster phallus they
want to jam down our throats. I am *furious* that
anyone would dare to suggest we'd consent to that
thing sitting on Park Avenue. Why, it's the most
beautiful avenue in New York, just as beautiful as
the Champs-Elysées in Paris!"

"As beautiful as what, Joe?"

"The Champs-Elysées, dummy!"

"What kinda champs?"

"Get off the phone, phony!"

Next a woman spoke: "Good morning, Joe
Shmoe."

"Yes, what is it, madame?"

"I just wanted to tell you that you're a jerk!"

"Thank you, madame."

Joe paused for a drink of water; his sound effects man amplified the sound, then added the roar of a waterfall.

"I needed that. Now let's see who's on the line. Hello sir or madame or anything in-between, are you there?"

"Joe . . . about the obelisk to the city . . ."

"You mean the gobble-risk, sir. Gobble, gobble, gobble . . . it's a real turkey."

"I think you're the funniest man alive, Joe, I listen to you all the time no matter what I'm doing."

"Don't lie to me, you bum!"

"Why should I lie to you, Joe? You make me laugh all the time and what's more I think you're doing a good job for guys like me who aren't heard."

"Look, stupid, you don't have to butter me up. You have as much influence as I do. I'm just one guy on the radio, but you're a few million out there where it counts. *You have influence. . . . Use it!*" Call the Parks, Recreation, and Cultural Affairs Administration. Let them know your views. They have not yet taken a final position on the monument. Get your friends to call if you have any."

"Yes, but Joe, can I ask you a question?"

"Go ahead."

"What?"

"I said go ahead. Go on, ask your question."

"Oh, yeah, well . . . what makes you think that homosexuals are behind this statue?"

"Aren't they behind everything?"

"I don't get you, Joe."

"The funniest man you ever heard was making a joke, a witticism, jerk, but it went right over your head. I won't bother to explain, sir, it would be blipped right off the air."

"Have you ever been approached by a homo, Joe? I was wondering what you would do if it happened?"

"I'd punch his nose down his throat that's what I'd do! What do you think I'd do? Isn't the city contaminated enough?"

"I agree, I agree, baby, I'd do the same thing."

"You sound like a pansy yourself, sir. Are you gay?"

"Cross my heart, Joe, I'm not. I'm a fireman."

"A fireman? You expect me to believe that? You want me to believe that you handle the hose, give mouth-to-mouth resuscitation. . . . What do you do with your time in the firehouse?"

"You got me wrong, Joe. I don't do nothing but play cards, cook, sleep. . . ."

"When do you see your wife, may I ask?"

"I'm not married, Joe."

"Ahha! Not married! And you want me to believe you're okay?"

"I called you to have a friendly conversation, Joe, not to be insulted."

"I'm the one who's insulted, *fag*! Get off the line and don't come back. I'll remember your voice, your *fag* voice!"

The sound effects man brought on the sound of

a huge explosion, and then I heard a tiny whimper before Joe spoke again.

"Ladies and gentlemen, I know when I'm being put on. My last caller was a representative of the most odious, insidious group of people in the world —a homosexual. I wouldn't have minded his call if he had stood up like a man and admitted that he was a *homo* . . . but he had to come sneaking around like a thief in the night trying to fool me. Well, I can't be fooled. *They* want equal rights, but they are not equal, they are *less than* human. If any one of them would call in and say, 'Joe, I can't help it, I'm sick,' we might have the beginning of a dialogue, but they come on as if they are healthy, happy people, just like you and me. Would you want one of these vipers in *fag* clothing to teach *your* child right from wrong? Would you want one of these vile piles of garbage to dump themselves in your home just because the law says you *must*? They are weak, they are sick, they are perverted, and they know it. They want everyone to be like them—barren human beings. I'd deport every one of them if I could, and then they'd be with their own kind. Folks, these scum want the human race to die out. Do you? *Do you?* They have reduced the sacred sexual act to exactly that . . . an act . . . often an act of sodomy . . . and in their desperation they would take your children. Please. *Please* demonstrate against the bill for equal rights for gay people. They are not only gay, they are hilarious, and this monument they propose will turn out to be a private club for gays, mark my word. It will become the most expensive pissoir on Park Avenue. The stench will drive out respectable people. It will float from Ninety-sixth Street to Grand Central Terminal. *Homos! Gays! Go back where you came from, the gutters, the sewers!* Oh, they're driving me mad. Lucky for me I'm about to depart for my semiannual trip to Tahiti, where the coconut milk still flows and pretty maidens all in a raw will sway their pretty hips in grass skirts for me. I'm going to Tahiti, where a man who is a *man* can still find peace, beauty, and natural sex . . . and you can go, too, friends, if you'll just call this number. . . ."

"Hello Joe?"

"Yes, stupid, who'd you think it was?"

"Joe, I hope you get leprosy and syphilis in Tahiti!"

"There it is, friends, you heard it here. When in doubt they call names. They don't know how to fight fair."

"Joe?"

"Yes, madame, this is Joe Shmoe on the line. Can I help you?"

"Listen, Joe, my father is not a fag and he's the person who proposed the monument. It is not a phallic symbol, it is more of an androgynous plant having both male and female organs. By a miracle of nature the bee fertilizes this flower and causes it to reproduce itself. This has nothing to do with

homosexuality. God made the trees, the flowers, and
he made me. Thank you."

95 "You're not grasping what I'm saying," Myra said on the telephone from Edward's
house. "Edward is dead, and I want you to come
right over."

I felt nothing. I thought I felt nothing. I would
require evidence. I still had things to settle with
Daddy; he couldn't have died.

"I've got to wash and dress, Myra; I got up late."

"You're a cold fish," Myra said accusingly.

"You want me to fall apart on the telephone?"
I asked.

"Aren't you even going to ask how it happened?"

"Later Mother, later."

96 First Pablo, now Father. Is Pablo
really a dog, or is he a sign? I often make tragic
mistakes. How to interpret disappearances? How
far I am from those I love!

97

Edward had developed a severe asthma in reaction to plant pollen. It may be true that all men kill the one they love, but it is equally true that loved ones frequently murder those who care for them. Destruction is distressingly reciprocal. Edward would not send his plants away, though he knew close proximity to them would be his doom. Before his death he had been involved in a number of "blind" experiments in order to effect a single cure for a number of ailments. His incentive was that what may *seem* to be an impenetrable maze, may presently bring one out into the light. The bulk of his experiments were not made in a haphazard manner but were attained by experimentation along rigidly predetermined lines. He wanted to break through the expected, to be surprised; he had begun to be influenced by the creative artist's use of chance. During our last visit together, Edward had said: "I recall reading an address by the late Professor Newton, a distinguished astronomer, on the subject of 'dead work,' in which he emphasized the fact that many of the experiments which any scientific worker must make will lead to no definite goal. . . ."

Edward was cremated and his ashes strewn over Burbank, California, which was what he wanted. Ashes to flowers, trees, and fruit. To remain a healer even in death.

98   At the services, all the things said about Daddy were true and beautiful, about his courage and faith, his difficulties, and the persecution he had to put up with because of the medical profession's prejudice. Following is a eulogy by his friend. R. D. Reeuw, M.R.C.S. . . L.R.C.P.

"I first met Edward Jones at the International Homeopathic Congress in 1936. This meeting was the beginning of a friendship lasting until the day of his death. During those years I had the privilege of keeping in touch with him either personally or by letter, and in this way sharing with him each new discovery.

"One characteristic of his work was his unselfish desire to help humanity; he wanted nothing for himself. He refused payment for his treatments, and gave away the clothes off his back. The finding of each new remedy filled him with joy and thankfulness to the Giver of all. He considered himself only as the instrument through which the remedies came.

"Jones has gone from our sight, but his work lives on, and only those who worked with him know the great value of his discoveries."

99 Myra held a séance to call Edward back. In the solemn stillness we waited for three notes on a trumpet to be sounded. "He will announce himself," Myra promised, "but we must be very quiet."

Quiet or not, there was no trumpet.

Myra said, "It must be in use elsewhere. I'll try reaching him directly." She stared into a corner of the darkened room. "Edward, my love, if you are here reveal yourself."

"How can he do that?" I whispered restlessly. I had had enough of fakery. Edward was certainly beyond the limits of stark, raving reality. He was dead and spread over the toasted terrain of Burbank.

"Listen, he is here."

I listened and heard three distinct thumps against some kind of resonant wood.

"Is it you, Edward? Knock twice if it is you," Mother asked hopefully.

This time the thumps were reduced by one.

A blurred and dissolving form detached itself from the ceiling. At first it was aimless, then it settled above Mother.

A scent of mildew and incense, so faint that it seemed to come from another dimension, entered my nostrils. Impetuously I cried out: "Daddy!" The blurred form descended and embraced me. Its cloudy, armlike protuberances drifted around me like clouds. Smoke made my eyes tear. Spots were swimming in them. I began to feel faint. There was a crash as Myra dropped her braceleted arm to the table.

"Something's burning!" she said before passing out.

Using the chair in which she was slumped as a stretcher, I dragged her out of the apartment and into the hall. Firemen were already rushing up the stairs, and I could hear the breaking of glass as other firefighters, coming up a ladder, hatcheted the windows. We hadn't been in there long enough to suffer smoke poisoning, but we had inhaled more smoke than was healthy. A neighbor remarked that he had seen our old friend Albert around the building. Too bad we had missed him.

100

I'm rich. Now what'll I do? Daddy left me his house and almost all of his money. There is one stipulation: I must spend at least three days out of the week helping people or I don't get the $. What constitutes helping? If I ball people who want me, is that helping? If I read stories to orphans and take them to the playground, is that helping? If I give a drunk a lifetime supply of sen-sen and gin, is that helping? Or must I play cards with the geriatric crowd and get them to smile? No, Daddy, you can't trick me into a useful life so that your death will seem useful.

What I think I'd like to do is move furniture. Sweat it out. Bend and lift. Shove and carry. Exhaust myself. I'm so tired of resting. (What do you think Edward?)

What I think I'd like to do is get in touch with Joe Fafka. Win friends and influence people. Have power and my own money. (What do you think Edward?)

What I think I'd like to do is write an article for *Cosmopolitan* about a three-way: mother, daughter, father. Yes, I'll use Joe Fafka's influence to contact the articles editor. (What do you think Edward?)

101
No sooner said than done! A reply from *Cosmo*.

Dear Helen,

I'm delighted you're going to do "Family as Lovers." As agreed, we see it as a major four-thousand-word article and can pay $1,000.00 for an accepted manuscript with a $100.00 write off if disaster strikes (which it won't).

THE COSMOPOLITAN GIRL

I'm enclosing some notes. Call me if you have any questions.

My best,
Daisy Roberts
Articles Editor

102 *FAMILY AS LOVERS*

Article simply discussing incestuous relationships . . . Do close relations make good lovers?

this is a bit spurious since some are going to be bad and some of them good—like ALL lovers—but it will be an interesting subject and well read.

whereas cosmo is AGAINST incest and respects the old taboos perhaps we have been too harsh—and cliché in our own thinking—

the artical might have a humorous approach
    or a serious approach—
        probably a little of both
    use attached article for fodder
        writer should know
        others who have family sex,
        article shouldn't be just her own
        experiences—
needs more general approach than that . . .

103 Article going well. Already have four typewritten pages.

104 Article going well. Already have three typewritten pages.

105 Article may not be written. Should be able to begin on the fifteenth page, as one begins on the top floor of the Guggenheim to see the show. It's too exhausting to begin on page one. It's never any good. Has anything ever been written backward?

106 .reverof em evarc mih ekam dluohs amleS hserf fo etsat teews eht, ffo repparw ym sleep luaP nehw, nehT. wollamarc a ekil nat ni depparw nruter ll'I.

DNE

107

Hearing the sound of a dog barking, I give a slight start and am more moved than ever. I bite my underlip. In front of the flower shop at the side entrance of the Buckminster, two dogs are playing. One is leashed, the other free. I stop to look at the dogs with great tenderness. Sharply etched against the side of the building is a grouping of flowers that is swaying in the wind. The vagrant dog runs away. Seen in profile, the tethered dog is me.

Dream fragment: 5 A.M. Wed. Day.

108

Edward willed one hundred thousand dollars to research, to establish the existence of a plant soul. The will said that aside from funeral expenses, money for an old clerical friend to say good-bye at the grave, and what should go to me and Myra, the rest of the money should be given "for research or some other scientific proof of a soul of a flower, or other plant, which leaves at death."

"I think there can be a photograph of a soul leaving the flower at death," said the will, which was declared legal.

About one hundred and forty groups and individuals laid claim to the money, and in June, Judge Martin ruled that the fortune should go to the Homeopathetique Botanical Institute of East Orange, New Jersey.

The New Jersey-based society has fourteen hundred members and "studies crisis apparitions, deathbed visions, and out-of-plant experiences." It claims to have had extraordinary success with vascular plants in particular.

109

Now that Myra was my only living relative, I had the desire to be close to her . . . but certain matters, unhappy childhood traumas, would have to be brought out in the open first. My letter to her, though harsh, was intended as a wedge in the door.

Mommy,

Nothing is easy, and yet it IS easy. My love for you exists in spite of what you have done. Some memories are more important than others. Let me sort them out: your idea of a good time for me (for instance). When I was four years old, you put me on an amusement park ride. I stood in a big drum, you above it on a catwalk for observers.

The drum began to revolve, and as it accelerated, the bottom, on which my feet rested, dropped out. Because of centrifugal force I became plastered to the inner curve of the drum. I was terrified, could barely breathe . . . a smile of terror on my face. Toward the end of the ride, as I slid down slowly into what I believed to be a bottomless pit, the drum slackened its pace and the floor came up. You asked me how I liked the ride. Was malice intended?

You treated me worse than prisoners at the San Diego jail. Kept me in an all-concrete section of our home, with no windows, and only pumped air to breathe. The only time I saw daylight was when I went to the roof on Sundays (Edward was away most of the time attending conferences or on field trips, so he was in ignorance of how you abused me. You also threatened to kill me if I told). My constant question to you was: "Is the sun shining outside or not?"

When you were despondent over losing a lover, you asked me to kill you with a butcher knife. I refused to do so. You then took a light bulb out of a socket, cocked the hammer of your .38 caliber revolver, handed me the gun and commanded me to shoot you while you had your finger in the light socket. (What you did not know was that I had flipped the light switch off, but there was no way for me to empty the gun before I pointed it at you.) You then asked me for a glass of water. You held it and sipped. I pulled the trigger of the gun. It misfired. Hysterically you fell upon a nearby couch. I covered you with a blanket. When you awoke you denied everything. It was as if I had dreamed it.

I know you meant well, but I'm scarred for life.

Now that we understand each other (now that you are old and the shoe is on the other foot), I intend to show you what loving kindness is. I want to be helpful. I am inviting you to come and live with me in Edward's house until the bitter end. There will be no reprisals.

Helen Jones

110 A curt note from Myra: "Do you realize what it's like to hear the horrible tramping of little feet in heavy boots? And to watch your pinched face, tiny ass, wee beastie breasties, all cute and mean so deadly earnest at thirteen?—*Mommy*

111 So that's the way she wants to play.

112 I have not reconciled the two aspects of my character: the animal and the human. No, they are at war. Whenever I want something intensely, I consider myself animal or instinctive; when I manage to repress my desires—sex, violence, hunger—it is then that I regard myself as a human being.

113 Mr. Fafka invited me to be his co-host on a program concerning mistaken identity. It is chilling to think that even I might be pulled off the street at any time and arrested just because I happen to resemble a crime suspect. I do carry about with me a vague guilt for having done something bad . . . but what?

114

"Yes sir," Joe said, "if you have a story to tell us, go ahead, we're waiting."

"I'm calling from the Tombs, Joe. I'm innocent. There's another guy out there, walking free, who is the spitting image of me. I'm no murderer. I'm gonna sue the city!"

"You mean you're calling *me* instead of your lawyer, stupid?"

"Yeah, Joe."

"How do you expect *me* to help you?"

"I dunno."

"Well then, blow this out of your barracks bag, creep. . . . You're a contemptible, cretinous, character of the lowest caliber, you're a twisted knife in the side of humanity, a cyanide bullet in the brain of innocence, you're a raging maniac who was easily identified in the police lineup, am I right so far?"

"Yes, Joe."

"And you have a previous record as long as a city block, don't you?"

"Right on the button, Joe."

"Then why are you wasting our time with this nonsense?"

"Nonsense?"

"*Nonsense.* Take your punishment like a man, jerk! I hope they string you up by your shoelaces so you choke to death. May you drink water out of a toilet bowl for the rest of your unnatural life and may you find maggots in your meat forever and ever amen! Excuse me while I weep with rage, friends."

"You've made me feel much better, Joe. Before I called you I was living a lie; I couldn't face up to what I was and what I done. Now the whole world knows I'm rotten and I'm ready to take the rap. God bless you, Mr. Fafka."

"My pleasure," Joe answered. He gave me a reassuring nod and took another call; the accent was unmistakenly British.

"Good morning, sir."

"Sir *Fafka* if you please, madame, Mrs. Fancy Frump! Where'd you pick up that way of talking?"

"I was born in Great Britain, Mr. Fafka."

"Madame, I'll bet you were born in the Bronx and took a cram course with Mr. Jeeves at the American Academy of Dramatic Arts."

"Joe, I called in to tell you that I've often been mistaken for Elizabeth Taylor . . . even by Richard Burton."

Joe got rid of her fast. "Why do the kooks call me?" he screamed. "If there are any sane people out there, please talk to me before I go bananas."

"Mr. Fafka, I heard your cry for help. There's nothing wrong with me, but I think you're nuts."

"Next!" Joe said.

"I am so happy to be talking to you, Joe. You don't have any idea. How's about you dropping by my house the next time you're in Oshawashkee, Missouri?"

"You've called me long distance, ma'am. Why me?"

"I love you, Joe, that's why. Every night I say a little prayer for you."

"Would you mind saying it for me now?"

"Not at all. Dear God who are in Heaven, bless Joe Fafka for all the happiness he brings to us shut-ins, and protect him from sorrow and pain. When finally You and he meet, oh Lord, I hope You'll introduce me. Amen."

"Thank you for your kind thought, madame, and . . ."

"Joe, I want to comment on a recent strange experience. Just yesterday, as I was sitting in my wheelchair, I was mistaken for Golda Meir by two Arabs who kept me in a locked room for six hours. But no matter what they did I refused to return the Wailing Wall."

"I can't take it! I can't take it!" Joe screamed. "Helen, I'll talk to you."

"Sure, Joe, talk to me."

"Helen, don't you think that most people feel as if they are victims of mistaken identity? Why do you think there are sex changes, transvestites, Jesus Christs, and Napoleons in the world?

"Because the grass is always greener on the other side of the fence?"

"Wrong! It's because nobody wants to face re-

sponsibility. I've spoken to a number of Jesus
Christs in my day and they all seem to be living on
past glories; the Bible's been written and they're
satisfied to rest on their laurels. The same with the
Napoleons: they're not interested in catacombs,
sewage systems, or war. All they want to do is to
stand around with one hand stuck in their jacket.
It's narcissistic. It's all for show—Hold your
thought, Helen, there's another call coming in . . .
Yes? . . . This is for you, Helen."

"Miss Jones . . ." The voice was a familiar one:
rough gutteral, something between a whimper and a
bark. "For years now I've been mistaken for a dog.
Because I was treated like a dog, I began to have a
dog's mentality. Unless I get some help this is the
end of the road for me, the end of a dusty, lonely
road."

"Please give your name to the operator when
I say 'now,' sir. You are not allowed to speak your
name on the air. Okay . . . now!" Joe said.

115 I found Pablo holed up in a thirty-
dollar-a-week fleabag hotel on the Bowery, living
on frankfurters and three cheap movies a day. I
didn't have to plead too hard to take him home
with me. He had spent practically his last dime on

the phone call to Joe Fafka. I took him to Edward's house, fed him, bathed him, bedded him—all without reproach. But for months he didn't respond. He was like a vegetable.

"What happened to you, Pablo?"

"Luis Farash didn't give me a cent . . . and he's disappeared. Gone to the mid-East with a show. At least I'm not fat any more."

"Why do you say you're not a dog, Pablo? Men don't have tails."

"Look. Neither do I."

He was right, Luis Farash had gotten Pablo a tail job.

"Maybe you are a man," I said.

"I am."

"I'll help you rebuild your life as a man."

"And then we'll get married."

116
One should not discuss a dream in front of a simpleton.

117
Word of Albert reached me via the news. He's roaming free again. The caption—LOUD LAUGHER GOES FREE—meant Albert. I read: "Traf-

fic court judge Viola Ramsey granted Albert Onestein the last laugh by dismissing charges against
him of 'laughing in a loud voice' aboard a bus. An
off-duty policewoman, who had recently overcome
deafness by a near miracle, testified that Mr. Onestein had refused to stop what she called 'a wild
laugh' and so she had arrested him on a charge of
disorderly behavior. The judge, who could not even
get a smile out of Mr. Onestein, much less an
example of his disorderly 'wild laugh,' said the case
was 'ridiculous, and the charges have no foundation.' "

118
Joe told his audience that he is get-
ting a laser beam to sterilize all black men on welfare. He is also doubling his guard at the station.
Threats against him keep coming in. He seems to
thrive on danger.

"Let 'em come and get me! I'm ready for 'em!"
he said.

119   I'm going to be married in white, a double-ring ceremony. However, Pablo doesn't have any fingers so I'm giving him a gold bracelet for his right paw. Neither of us has a large guest list; on my side there's Mother, James McCrory, Albert, Marian & Jeremy, and Joe Fafka. On Pablo's side there's a feisty neighborhood pug he met outside the supermarket, Luis Farash (whom we've forgiven), and a snag-toothed bitch he claims is his real mother.

120   Instead of going to a pet store for Pablo's wedding gifts I wandered around town picking up things he might never use. I wasn't sure whether or not to satisfy his fantasy that he is a man. For instance, what would he do with a Hermes tie? Drag it across the floor? And that language record for his trip to France . . . he barely speaks his own language. As for his supposed mother (who is shedding and has dandruff), I thought of sending her a whirligig wire salad basket because they're fabulous and she doesn't have one, or, what might be more suitable since she has litter after litter, Sesame Street records for her pups.

121 Marian has RSVP'd regrets, although she and Jeremy have sent me a floor-length denim apron to wear with nothing under it at my next dinner for two. I think she is disappointed in me.

122 Dear Marian,
I'm sorry you won't be able to attend the wedding, but I want you to know that I am getting married to Pablo because I truly love him and because we have formed an alliance against those of you who think you know the way things should be. Living with Pablo will be the ultimate in gracious sexual living. . . . I won't have to use the Pill, or anything else . . . no backup system . . . no diaphragm, gel, foam, or abstinence. Take my word for it.

Love,
Helen

123 Dear Helen,
Then you intend to be faithful to Pablo?
Love,
Marian

124 Dear Marian,

If I slept with another male and had a child, it would be obvious that it wasn't Pablo's.

Love,
Helen

125 Dear Helen,

How dreary. Why do you want to take yourself out of the swim?

Love,
Marian

126 Dear Marian,

I'm afraid of drowning.

Love,
Helen

127 Dear Helen,

I don't believe you.

Love,
Marian

128 Dear Marian,
You're right. Things are liable to change. They always do. I am interested in another man. His name is Joe Fafka. Ring a bell? But he's the scum of the earth. Why do I always fall for the underdog?

Love,
Helen

129 Dear Helen,
Try the ménage à trois. I know that Pablo is poor, unemployed . . . a student of life . . . that beautiful waif you rescued from death, but face up to it, you'll be taking him in and paying for *everything,* while he stirs up trouble or blames you for his lack of success. He'll never admit it's his fault. You as sorcerer's apprentice will have to do what women have always had to do, brew up all kinds of magic to make him feel *he* is firmly in charge. Man, I can already hear you stifling those martyred sighs, saying to him: "I knock myself out all week to keep you in sirloin and you won't even heel, or beg on

command when guests are here," or, "Is that why I paid the vet fifty dollars . . . so you could act in a pornographic movie on the sly?" Please Helen, don't, at the expense of your own peace of mind give him his own checking account to cover bus fare, beer, his subscription to *Dogromp,* or anything else he says he needs. Don't merge at the bank, or put his name on the buzzer or mailbox. Before long he'll want to be top-dog: he'll take over and you'll be on the leash. Take it from a friend, you're gonna have trouble like you've never had before. Some of your most shattering battles are going to be over such trivialities as hair on the floor and in the bath, kibbles that have fallen between the couch pillows, and garbage that has soaked through the bag. A dog can't help but be a slob.

So that's why, dear friend, I suggest another man to keep you sane and happy. Extramural activity is necessary though it may be the grossest gluttony. In your case it's a decided necessity.

Love,
Marian

130 Dear Marian,
I think you're an absolute shit. But thanks anyway.

Love,
Helen

131 There is no chance at all that I will find Joe Fafka more irresistible than Pablo, though with him I will once again enjoy the world of lobster and Chablis.

132 Mother married us since we could not find a priest or reverend to agree on the marriage. Even homosexuals can be married in church now, but not woman and dog. No sanctification for us.

133 We knelt on red velvet cushions during the ceremony.
"Do you, Helen, take this creature to be your

lifelong companion, in distemper and mange, in cheerful mood and good health, till that Great Dog Catcher in the sky do you part?" the Reverend Jones asked.

"I do," I whispered shyly.

Mother turned to Pablo: "Do you, Pablo, take Helen as your wife, to have and to hold, and do you promise to lie down on command, come when called, and protect her life and limb to the best of your ability till death do you part?"

"I do," Pablo replied.

"Then with the power invested in me by myself and a God of my own choosing, I pronounce you hound and bitch and may you take your place among the great lovers of the world—Heloise and Abelard, Wally and Edward, Mickey and Minnie, Tarzan and Jane, Victoria and Albert, Jean-Paul and Simone, Molly and Leopold, Oscar and Alfred, Gertrude and Alice, Jack and Jill, Mick and Bianca, Allen and Peter, Henry and Nancy, Richard and Elizabeth, Paulo and Francesca, Dick and Bebe, Catherine the Great and? . . . You may now kiss each other."

First Pablo sniffed under my dress, then he slobbered all over my face. It was a moment I'll never forget. Though I was afraid he'd get worms I let him eat half the wedding cake, including the tiny bride and groom made of almond paste that stood at the top of the cake. When Joe Fafka congratulated me and kissed me on the lips Pablo growled. He was so jealous that he wouldn't allow me to pet him. "The human hand is an instrument of punishment," he said.

I hope it is not the beginning of the end.

134 Mother installed a bidet in the master bathroom as our wedding gift. She had just made a killing in the stock market.

"How did you do it, Mother? Everybody else is losing their shirts."

"I do it by relaxing my mind and letting visions drift into it," she said, "but first I sit on the latest copy of the *Wall Street Journal* for ten minutes, to absorb information. After a while I might see a bear riding on top of a bull, for instance, and in the background, there might be a company trademark. This would show me the company's stock price is about to fall. Sometimes Edward sends me messages. The only times I buy or sell are when I have those dreams and he tells me what to do."

"How is Dad?"

"We never discuss what he's doing or how he is."

"Does he ever mention me?"

"He mentioned Pablo."

"What did he say?"

"He said that someday a dog will be President,

and then he uttered something so cryptic that even **I** could not interpret it. He said: "To the victor the onions!"

"To the victor the onions?" I repeated. "Must have something to do with tears." I left it at that.

135 Joe Fafka is taking his vacation *chez moi* avec Pablo *aussi.* I once had a French lover who taught me how to say lots of things with *chez moi,* such as *Voulez-vous couchez avec moi chez moi?* I don't remember too much of it, but it used to turn him on. Anyway, Joe would never have come to me if he hadn't reached the breaking point; not only were his callers becoming dumber and dumber, but his home was burglarized and his most treasured possessions stolen.

JOE FAFKA LOSES GAME
BURGLAR TAKES PADDLES

While a well-known radio personality slept in his rented Manhattan duplex early yesterday, a burglar made off with more than $15,000 worth of loot. He took the celeb's most treasured possessions—six Ping-Pong paddles.

He was asleep in his second floor bedroom

when the burglar forced the kitchen window and entered the apartment.

When Fafka awoke and came downstairs around 6 A.M., he noticed that his stereo set had disappeared. Then he opened a living room closet and found that a special suitcase containing a model for a laser beam also was missing.

Meanwhile his maid discovered that his wallet, containing several credit cards but no cash, had vanished from the kitchen table where he had left it under the tablecloth the night before.

Fafka was most upset over the loss of his paddles, which he says were given to him by Xaviera Hollander when she appeared as a guest on his program. They are unusual paddles with wooden handles and rubber sponge faces and measure more than eight inches across.

"They aren't worth very much to anyone else," Fafka explained, "but to me they're priceless. They fit my hand perfectly and have just the right feel. I'll miss them." When pressed as to what he used them for, since they were too large for Ping-Pong, Mr. Fafka declined to explain.

136 The three of us—Joe, Pablo, and myself—play anagrams in the evening. Pablo always loses, yet he smiles. It is a strange smile . . . almost a threat.

"Why can't you be a good loser?" I asked. "You're full of hate."

"My hatred springs from the impossibility of my winning. Why don't you ever play games that are suited to my particular kind of intelligence?"

"What game for instance?" I asked.

"A game that employs the sense of smell, for instance: the game of Find the Bone. I am able to locate a bone that's been buried for as long as five years. . . . You wouldn't have a chance there."

137 It's Joe's fault that our life together has not been private and tranquil. Last week he announced that Daddy's favorite acacia tree had begun to cry. He described what happened as a miracle and with tongue in cheek predicted that the house on Sutton Place would become as holy a shrine as Lourdes.

"Yes, friends, trees too snivel and blubber all over the place. You've got to see it to believe it. My landlady tells me that the sap of the acacia tree can cure internal hemorrhages and that the water from her tree, which is at this moment wasting its tears, can cure anything."

People who wanted miraculous cures began calling. "Joe, my mother suffers from heart trouble. Should I bring her in from Monterey?"

"It's worth a try, isn't it, sonny?"

"It's very expensive, Joe."

"Then don't bring her, stingy!"

That was how it began, but soon people found out where we lived and parked outside till I let them in. Small boys collected water from the tree and sold it at fifty cents a drink from stands set up outside. In five days, three thousand unfortunate people passed through the house: an elderly lady with paralyzed arms (which she raised for a second after drinking some of the acacia water), a woman whose hands had been drawn into claws by arthritis, a child who'd been blind from birth, a victim of cancer whose jaw was eaten away, an opera diva who had lost her voice, a sixteen-year-old boy with acne, and so on. Finally I had to put up a ten-foot link fence right in my own living room, and the artwork went into storage. Pablo wanted to charge admission, but a visiting priest from Ecuador said, "This is God's tree, and this living room is holy."

People began to knock each other down in their efforts to get through the gates to the tree. Those who fell began to claw the mud around the roots, eating it and rubbing it on their afflicted parts. A young man was almost crushed to death between the fence and the TV.

Finally, Joe spoke up on the radio. "Friends, how can you conduct yourselves in such a selfish and vicious manner? I understand that this is a clear case of magical thinking, the kind that built cathedrals and fulfilled man's dreams, but your hope is misplaced. The tree is a fake. I repeat that: *the tree is a fake!* On careful analysis by government inspectors we have been apprised that there is nothing but filthy water coming out of a rotten knothole that's crusted over with crud. It makes me sick, *sick* to think people are drinking that stuff and putting it into their eyes and private parts. Cease and desist, I beg of you. It was a terrible mistake."

In a few days our enterprising neighbors who had opened soft-drink stands, snow-cone stands, and sandwich and popcorn concessions had left.

The incident injured Joe's credibility.

"Mr. Fafka, I think you're a rat giving hope and then taking it away."

"What is wrong with you, sir?"

"I'm dead from the waist down, Joe."

"And from the waist up too, jerk! I hope you stay paralyzed!"

"I don't drink, Joe."

"Liar! I can hear that fuzzy, blurry inflection in your voice, and I know, sir, that you are calling me in an alcoholic haze. If I ever hear your voice again I'll come get you wherever you are and tear your tongue out. You hear? Low life, lily-livered drunk! May you freeze on the Bowery next Christmas. . . . Well, folks, I guess that's telling him, and now for those of you who are planning a party or celebration

of some sort, Strawberry Cooler is the drink for you,
made from natural ingredients and containing only
eighteen percent alcohol. . . ."

138 I've got a superglamorous career now:
three days a week I take over for Joe. I handle the
calls more humanly, try not to insult potential
suicides or incite silent America to riot. I also ad-
vise people on sex and food although I do not have
the credentials of a Mazie Justins who wrote eighty-
seven pornographic novels before she went into the
advice columnist business and managed to spark her
helpful hints on multiple orgasm with wit and humor.
I do not have the credentials of an Emma Roget
who in her book on Italian regional cooking managed to mine from each of the fourteen main re-
gions recipes that had never before appeared in any
cookbook. But it is better to *not* be an expert in this
constantly changing universe; it is better to be sympathetic, ambiguous, and to give a number of
answers to a single question. Any recipe for living
or cooking must have a substitute list of ingredients:
when it is done, who can tell the difference anyway?

139 I no longer hang around the house with my clothes off. Joe the prude doesn't like it. Pablo adores it. He is sure that if I expose my body long enough I will grow a fine body of hair and then look more like him. He thinks that clothes press one's follicles shut, forcing the hair to grow inward, and that humans are being injured internally by bristly vibrissa which makes them nasty to other creatures. Whenever Pablo hides my clothes, Joe beats him. I don't know how to handle the situation. It's so explosive. Every time I go to work I'm afraid that the two men in my life will kill one another.

140 So much has happened since I've been on the air: a camera crew is coming to live with us to film our new life-style: the menagerie a trois. They will be with us for at least two months. I have my own lavaliere mike which hangs between my breasts—like the cross, or the Jewish star, or even the Egyptian ankh. It is symbolic of a religion, and looks very sexy. When Joe and Pablo catch sight of it they stop fighting.

141 One month into the filming. We do not hold a conversation unless the camera is going. A permanent floodlight has been installed in the bathroom, and one wall removed. There is a catwalk above the living room. Yesterday when I opened the oven door to make some biscuits I found a cameraman inside. He is a Maoist and has been photographing my jewels, furs, and silverware. Whenever we eat he takes close-ups of our mouths and what we leave over. He says he is making a political film.

142 The Maoist has been won over. I fed him a plate of litchi nuts and he succumbed to the past. Now he is easier to get along with, although who can tell a man's heart when he is eating?

143 The movie, called *Three on a Matchress,* has been shown on educational TV and is an instant success. Pablo no longer hides his ears under his hat or strains for an upright position: he has come out of the closet. Saks has introduced the Pablo Look: men want to look like dogs. Hair shirts are "in," padded palms and soles de rigueur, wet noses chic, and fetch-and-carry is swiftly taking the place of golf and tennis. Language itself is undergoing a change: instead of saying, "You're making a mistake," people are using phrases such as, "You're barking up the wrong tree." But in spite of his notoriety, Pablo is still not allowed in restaurants and supermarkets. He particularly misses not being able to go to the movies or an off-Broadway show. We have hired a civil liberties lawyer and plan a test case to liberate all dogs from unjust laws.

To clarify the situation at home, I wrote up a domestic contract by which we must all abide:

THE JONES-PABLO-FAFKA
DOMESTIC AGREEMENT

1. PRINCIPLES
We reject the notion that the work that brings in more money is not more valuable. The ability to earn money, or the fact that one already has it, should carry more weight in a relationship. Those

who do not have money to contribute should do the dirty work and be subservient in every other way, including sexually. This is not as rigid as it seems since bad treatment provides great motivation to change things and to better oneself. If anyone balks, I, Helen Jones, have the right to kick them out.

2. JOB BREAKDOWN AND SCHEDULE
    (A) Mornings: Buying newspaper, making breakfast, making lunches, shopping. Every other week each male does all.
    (B) Afternoons: Free time for all: Joe may prepare his next day's script; Pablo may masturbate; I may take Polaroids of their activities.
    (C) Nighttime (after 6 P.M.). On Tuesday, Thursday, and Sunday Pablo will tuck me in and have person-to-person talks. Joe will do me on Monday, Wednesday, and Saturday. Friday is split between both of them, or I may just say "No."
    (D) Cleaning and laundering to be done by commercial laundry.
    (E) All statements to the press must be cleared through me, Helen Jones.

144 The domestic agreement was made to ignore. And we did. We decided that it was humorless and degrading to the manifest spirit of our troilism. Consequently the contract was shredded and put into the gerbil cage where it would do more good.

145 Unfortunately, one side effect of our new togetherness has been a distortion of sexual generosity. It has become compulsive and no longer joyous. We feel we owe it to one another to drift (aimlessly) from bed to bed; all this is accomplished under the guise of sexual freedom. We have tried every position together.

I long to be alone!

Monks are not to be pitied; they know the value of chanting their way into oblivion where nobody will bother them. I miss Albert because of his surprising trunkful of costume changes, though I suspect he will finally immolate himself in one of them. And I miss the seven dwarfs because they took care of the house. And I miss Pablo's being just a pet, and Joe's being a mad, disembodied voice that lived in a static-free box. If only I knew then what I know now. Why is life so complicated? Why can't I conduct myself *beautifully* on every occasion? I want to make it as simple as this: "I am hungry, I will eat; I am frightened and ill, I will take a dose of Mimulus."